The Boys
In the Band

A PLAY IN TWO ACTS

By Mart Crowley

SAMUEL FRENCH, INC.

45 WEST 25TH STREET   NEW YORK 10010
7623 SUNSET BOULEVARD HOLLYWOOD 90046
LONDON   TORONTO

THE BOYS IN THE BAND was first produced on the New York stage by Richard Barr and Charles Woodward, Jr., at Theatre Four on April 14, 1968.

CHARACTERS

MICHAEL .... *Kenneth Nelson*

DONALD .... *Frederick Combs*

EMORY .... *Cliff Gorman*

LARRY .... *Keith Prentice*

HANK .... *Laurence Luckinbill*

BERNARD .... *Reuben Greene*

COWBOY .... *Robert La Tourneaux*

HAROLD .... *Leonard Frey*

ALAN .... *Peter White*

Directed by Robert Moore

Designed by Peter Harvey

Production Stage Manager, Charles Kindl

The play is divided into two acts. The action is continuous and occurs one evening within the time necessary to perform the play.

DESCRIPTION OF CHARACTERS

MICHAEL: Thirty, average face, smartly groomed.

DONALD: Twenty-eight, medium blond, wholesome American good looks.

EMORY: Thirty-three, small, frail, very plain.

LARRY: Twenty-nine with a starkly simple sense of individual style and color in his clothes. Dark eyes, dark hair, extremely handsome.

HANK: Thirty-two, tall, solid, athletic, attractive.

BERNARD: Twenty-eight, Negro, tall, gaunt, nice-looking, dressed in Ivy-League clothes.

COWBOY: Twenty-two, light blond, muscle-bound, too pretty.

HAROLD: Thirty-two, dark, lean, strong limbs, unusual semitic face.

ALAN: Thirty, aristocratic Anglo-Saxon features.

The Boys in the Band

ACT ONE

There is no curtain. The LIGHTS come up on a smartly appointed duplex apartment in the East Fifties, New York, consisting of a living room and, on a higher level, a bedroom. Bossa nova MUSIC blasts from a phonograph. MICHAEL, *wearing a robe, enters from the kitchen, carrying a Scotch liquor bottle and one red rose in a vase. He crosses to set Scotch on the bar, moves to the Left table to place vase. He crosses to sofa and sits and starts ribbon on package. The front door BUZZER sounds.* MICHAEL *stops tying package, goes to door, pushes button to release outside building door and opens apartment door and turns off PHONOGRAPH as* DONALD *enters.* DONALD *is dressed in khakis and a Lacoste shirt, carrying an airlines zipper bag and a stack of books.* DONALD *drops his books on sofa.*

MICHAEL. Donald! You're about a day and a half early!

DONALD. The doctor cancelled! (DONALD *puts zipper bag at top of stairs.*)

MICHAEL. Cancelled! How'd you get inside? (*Looks out front door.*)

DONALD. The street door was open. (*As he comes back to sofa to pick up books and* MICHAEL *closes door.*)

MICHAEL. You wanna drink?

DONALD. (*Deposits his books on bar and sits Right end of sofa.*) Not until I've had my shower. I want something to work-out today—I want to try to relax and enjoy *something.*

MICHAEL. (*Comes to Left end of sofa.*) You in a blue funk because of the doctor?

DONALD. (*Returning.*) Christ, no. I was depressed long before I got *there*.

MICHAEL. Why'd the prick cancel?

DONALD. A virus or something. He looked awful.

MICHAEL. (*Goes to desk for shopping bag and returns to Left of sofa.*) Well, this'll pick you up. I went shopping today and bought all kind of goodies.—Sandalwood soap . . .

DONALD. (*Removing his sox and shoes.*) I feel better already.

MICHAEL. (*Producing articles.*) —Your very own toothbrush because I'm sick to death of your using mine.

DONALD. How do you think *I* feel.

MICHAEL. (*Holds up a cylindrical can and crosses to Right end of sofa.*) And, also for you . . . something called "Control." Notice nowhere is it called hair spray— just simply, "Control." And the words, "For Men," are written about thirty-seven times all over the goddamn can!

DONALD. It's called Butch Assurance.

MICHAEL. Well, it's *still* hair spray—no matter if they call it *"Balls"! (Goes above sofa, picks up bag and goes to step landing.*) It's all going on your very own shelf which is to be labeled: Donald's Saturday Night Douche Kit. (*Shouting over shoulder as he takes bag to bathroom on second level.*) By the way, are you spending the night?

DONALD. (*Shouting.*) Nope. I'm driving back. I still get very itchy when I'm in this town too long. I'm not that well yet.

MICHAEL. (*Enters from bath and crosses to landing and sits on railing.*) That's what you say every week end.

DONALD. Maybe after about ten more years of analysis I'll be able to stay one night.

MICHAEL. Maybe after about ten more years of analysis you'll be able to move back to town permanently.

DONALD. If I live that long.

MICHAEL. You will. If you don't kill yourself on the Long Island Expressway some early Sunday morning. I'll never know how you can tank-up on martinis and make it back to the Hamptons in one piece.

DONALD. (*Rises with shoes and socks and crosses to* MICHAEL.) Believe me, it's easier than getting here. Ever had an anxiety attack at sixty miles an hour? Well, tonight I was beside myself to get to the doctor—and just as I finally make it, rush in, throw myself on the couch and vomit-out how depressed I am, he says, "Donald, I have to cancel tonight—I'm just too sick." (*Starts to bathroom.*)

MICHAEL. Why didn't you tell him you're sicker than he is.

DONALD. He already knows *that*. (*Picks up bag and goes to bath where he leaves bag, shoes and so ks.*)

MICHAEL. Why didn't the prick call you and cancel? Suppose you'd driven all this way for nothing.

DONALD. (*Enters from bath to Right of bed.*) Why do you keep calling him a prick?

MICHAEL. Whoever heard of an analyst having a session with a patient for two hours on Saturday evening.

DONALD. He simply prefers to take Mondays off. (*Removing his shirt.*)

MICHAEL. Works late on Saturday and takes Monday off—what is he, a psychiatrist or a hairdresser?

DONALD. Actually, he's both. He shrinks my head and combs me out. (MICHAEL *enters bedroom and crosses to hair drier.*) Besides, I had to come in town to a birthday party anyway. Right? (*Sits on bed.*)

MICHAEL. You had to remind me. If there's one thing I'm not ready for, it's five screaming queens singing Happy Birthday. (*Winding up cord on drier and exits bath.*)

DONALD. Who's coming?

MICHAEL. (*Putting pants on in bath.*) They're really all Harold's friends. It's *his* birthday and I want everything to be just the way he'd want it. I don't want to have to listen to him kvetch about how nobody ever does anything for anybody but themself.

DONALD. Himself.

MICHAEL. I think you know everybody anyway— (*He enters from bath and crosses to* DONALD.) they're the same old tired fairies you've seen around since the day one. Actually, there'll be seven counting Harold and you and me.

DONALD. Are you calling me a screaming queen or a tired fairy?

MICHAEL. Oh, I beg your pardon—six tired screaming fairy queens and one anxious queer. (*Removes slippers and deposits Left side of bed.*)

DONALD. You don't think Harold'll mind my being here, do you? Technically, I'm *your* friend, not his.

MICHAEL. (*Crossing to bed table for comb.*) If she doesn't like it, she can twirl on it. Listen, I'll be out of your way in just a second. I've only got one more thing to do. (*He goes to mirror.*)

DONALD. Surgery, so early in the evening?

MICHAEL. (*Turns to* DONALD.) Sunt! That's French, with a cedilla. I've just got to comb my hair for the thirty-seventh time. Hair—that's singular. My hair, without exaggeration, is clearly falling on the floor. And *fast,* baby!

DONALD. You're totally paranoid. You've got plenty of hair.

MICHAEL. What you see before you is a masterpiece of deception. My hairline starts about here. (*Indicates his crown.*) All this is just tortured forward.

DONALD. Well, I hope for your sake, no strong wind comes up.

MICHAEL. If one does, I'll be in terrible trouble. I will then have a bald head and shoulder-length fringe. (*He runs his fingers through his hair, holds it away from his scalp, dips the top of his head so that* DONALD *can see.* DONALD *is silent.*) Not good, huh?

DONALD. Not the greatest.

MICHAEL. It's called, "getting old"— Well, one thing

you can say for masturbation—you certainly don't have to look your best. (*He slips out of the robe, flings it at* DONALD. DONALD *laughs, takes the robe, exits to the bath.* MICHAEL *takes a sweater from bed table and pulls it on.*) What are you so depressed about? I mean, other than the usual *everything*. (*At mirror checking hair.*)

DONALD. (*Reluctantly.*) Michael, I really don't want to get in o it.

MICHAEL. Well, if you're not going to tell me how can we have a conversation *in depth*—a warm, rewarding, meaningful friendship? (*Sits on bench and puts on shoes.*)

DONALD. Up yours!

MICHAEL. (*Southern accent.*) Why, Cap'n Butler, how you talk!

(DONALD *crosses to* MICHAEL *holding a glass of water with* MICHAEL'S *robe on and no pants.* MICHAEL *looks up.*)

DONALD. It's just that today I finally realized that I was *raised* to be a failure. I was *groomed* for it. (*Takes a pill.*)

MICHAEL. You know, there was a time when you could have said that to me and I wouldn't have known what the hell you were talking about.

DONALD. Naturally, it all goes back to Evelyn and Walt. (*Sits bedroom chair.*)

MICHAEL. Naturally. When doesn't it go back to Mom and Pop. Unfortunately, we all had an Evelyn and a Walt. The Crumbs! Don't you love that word—crumb? Oh, I love it! It's a real Barbara Stanwyck word. (*He rises. A la Stanwyck's frozen-lipped Brooklyn accent:*) "Cau"ll me a keab, you kr-rumm."

DONALD. Well, I see all vestiges of sanity for this evening are now officially shot-to-hell.

MICHAEL. (*Goes to* DONALD.) Oh, Donald, you're so serious tonight! You're fun-starved, baby, and I'm eating for two! (*Sings.*) "Forget your troubles, c'mon get happy! You better chase all your blues away. Shout, 'Hallelujah!'

c'mon get happy . . ."* (MICHAEL *does a few Garland poses. Sees* DONALD *isn't buying it.*) —what's more boring than a queen doing a Judy Garland imitation?

DONALD. (*Rises.*) A queen doing a Bette Davis imitation. (*Exits to bath, leaving glass.*)

MICHAEL. (*Goes to chair, sits and buffs shoes with mitt.*) Meanwhile—back at the Evelyn and Walt Syndrome.

DONALD. (*Crosses to* MICHAEL.) America's Square Peg and America's Round Hole.

MICHAEL. Christ, how sick analysts must get of hearing how mommy and daddy made their darlin' into a fairy.

DONALD. It's beyond just that now. Today I finally began to see how some of the other pieces of the puzzle relate to them.—Like why I never finished anything I started in my life . . . my neurotic compulsion to not succeed. I've realized it was always when I failed that Evelyn loved me the most—because it displeased Walt who wanted perfection. And when I fell short of the mark she was only too happy to make up for it with her love. (*Sits on bed.*) So I began to identify failing with winning my mother's love. And I began to fail on purpose to get it. I didn't finish Cornell—I couldn't keep a job in this town. I simply retreated to a room over a garage and scrubbing floors in order to keep alive. Failure is the only thing with which I feel at home. Because it is what I was taught at home.

MICHAEL. Killer whales. Killer whales is what they are. How many whales could a killer whale kill?

DONALD. A lot especially if they get them when they are babies. (*Pause.* MICHAEL *suddenly tears off his sweater, throws it in the air, letting it land where it may, goes to Left of bed and whips another sweater out pulls it on as*

---

*GET HAPPY by Ted Koehler and Harold Arlen. © 1929 by Remick Music Corp. Reprinted by permission of Warner Bros. Music. For permission to use this number in the production of this play apply to Warner Bros. Music, 488 Madison Ave. NYC. N.Y. 10022.

he starts for the living room. DONALD *follows.*) Hey! Where're you going? (*Stops on landing.*)

MICHAEL. (*Finishes putting sweater on at bar.*) To make drinks! I think we need about thirty-seven!

DONALD. Where'd you get *that* sweater?

MICHAEL. This clever little shop on the right bank called *Hermes.*

DONALD. I work my ass off for forty-five lousy dollars a week *scrubbing* floors and you waltz around throwing cashmere sweaters on them.

MICHAEL. The one on the floor in the bedroom is vicuna.

DONALD. I *beg* your pardon.

MICHAEL. You could get a job doing something else. Nobody holds a gun to your head to be a char-woman. That is, how you say, your neurosis.

DONALD. (*Sits on landing.*) Gee, and I thought it's why I was born.

MICHAEL. (*Goes to desk for scotch tape.*) Besides, just because I *wear* expensive clothes doesn't necessarily mean they're paid for.

DONALD. That is, how you say, *your* neurosis.

MICHAEL. (*Crosses to Center.*) I'm a spoiled brat so what do I know about being mature. The only thing mature means to me is *Victor* Mature who was in all those pictures with Betty Grable. (*Sings a la Grable.*) "I can't begin to tell you, how much you mean to me . . ." Betty sang that in 1945. (*Crosses to coffee table and puts tape by gift package.*) '45?—'43. No, '43 was "Coney Island" which was re-made in '50 as "Wabash Avenue." Yes, "Dolly Sisters" was in '45. (*Crosses to desk for scissors and bow.*)

DONALD. How did I manage to miss these momentous events in the American Cinema? I can understand people having an affinity for stage—but movies are such garbage, who can take them seriously?

MICHAEL. (*He is back to Center.*) Well, I'm sorry if your sense of art is offended. Odd as it may seem there was no Shubert Theatre in Hot Coffee, Mississippi! (*Crosses to sofa, sits and finishes ribbon tying.*)

DONALD. However—thanks to the silver screen, your neurosis has got style. (*Rises, crosses to* MICHAEL.) It takes a certain flair to squander one's unemployment check at Pavillion.

MICHAEL. What's so snappy about being head over heels in debt. The only thing smart about it is the ingenious ways I dodge the bill collectors.

(DONALD *helps* MICHAEL *to tie a knot with the use of his finger.*)

DONALD. Yeah. Come to think of it, you're the type that gives faggots a bad name.

MICHAEL. And you, Donald, *you* are a credit to the homosexual. A reliable, hard-working, floor-scrubbing, bill-paying fag who don't owe nothin' to nobody. (*Cuts off excess ribbon.*)

DONALD. *I* am a model fairy.

MICHAEL. (*Puffs up bow.*) You think it's just nifty how I've always flitted from Beverly Hills to Rome to Acapulco to Amsterdam— (DONALD *slowly goes above sofa, looks at phono and then to bar where he leans to listen.*) picking up a lot of one-night stands and a lot of custom-made duds along the trail, but I'm here to tell you that the only place in all those miles—the only place I've ever been *happy*—was on the goddamn plane. Bored with Scandinavia, try Greece. Fed up with dark meat, try light. Hate tequila, what about slivovitz? Tired of boys, what about girls?—or how about boys and girls mixed and in what combination? (DONALD *laughs and sits in Down Right chair.*) And if you're sick of people, what about poppers? Or pot or pills or the hard stuff. And can you think of anything else the bad baby would like to indulge his spoiled-rotten, stupid empty, boring, selfish, self-centered self in? (*Makes a scotch tape loop.*) Is that what you think has style, Donald? Huh? Is that what you think you've missed out on—my hysterical escapes from country to country, party to party, bar to bar, bed to bed, hang-over to hangover, and all of it, hand to mouth! (*Tape to package.*) Run, charge, run, buy, borrow, make, spend, run, squander, beg, run, run, run, waste, waste, *waste!* (*Bow to tape.*) And why? And why? (*Leans back on sofa.*)

DONALD. Why, Michael? Why?

MICHAEL. I really don't want to get into it.

DONALD. Then how can we have a conversation in depth?

MICHAEL. Oh, you know it all by heart anyway. Same song, second verse. Because my Evelyn refused to let me grow up. She was determined to keep me a child forever and she did one helluva job of it. And my Walt stood by and let her do it. (*A beat.*) What you see before you is a thirty-year-old infant. And it was all done in the name of love—what *she* labeled love and probably sincerely be-lieved to be love, when what she was really doing was feeding her own need—satisfying her own loneliness. (*Picks up cut-off ribbon and puts in ashtray.*) She bathed me in the same tub with her until I grew too big for the two of us to fit and she made me sleep in the same bed with her until I was fourteen years old—until I finally flatly refused to spend one more night there. And do you know until this day she still says, "I don't care if you're seventy years old, you'll always be my baby." (*Rises and crosses to* DONALD.) And can I tell you how that drives me mad! Will that bitch never understand that what I'll always *be* is her son—but that I haven't been her baby for twenty-five years! (*Picks up scissors and tape from coffee table and takes up to desk.*) And don't get me wrong. I know it's easy to cop out and blame Evelyn and Walt and say it was *their* fault. That we were simply the helpless put-upon victims. But I've dropped enough dough on the couch to know that in the end, you are responsible for yourself. (*Crosses to finished package on coffee table and picks up.*) And I guess—I'm not sure—but I want to believe it—that in their own pathetic, dangerous way, they just loved us too much. (*A beat.*) Finis. Applause. (DON-ALD *hesitates, walks over to* MICHAEL, *puts his arms around him and holds him. It is a totally warm and caring gesture.*) There's nothing quite as good as feeling sorry for yourself, is there?

DONALD. Nothing.

MICHAEL. (*A la Bette Davis.*) I adore cheap sentiment. (*Breaks away to steps, putting gift on fourth step.*) Okay, I'm taking orders for drinks. What'll it be?

DONALD. (*As going up stairs to bath.*) An extra-dry-Beefeater-martini-on-the-rocks-with-a-twist.

MICHAEL. Coming up. (DONALD *exits to the bath.* MICHAEL *starts to bar to make Donald's drink and notices there is no ice, so exits to kitchen singing "Acapulco." As he exits, the TELEPHONE rings on an empty Stage. Momentarily,* MICHAEL *returns, carrying an ice bucket in one hand and a tray of cracked crab in the other. He puts crab on coffee table and answers phone at desk.*) Back-stage, "New Moon." (*A beat.*) Alan? Alan! My God, I don't believe it. How *are* you? Where *are* you? In town! Great! When'd you get in? Is Fran with you? Oh. What? No. (*Crosses to bar with phone and ice, sets ice on bar.*) No, I'm tied-up tonight. No, tonight's no good for me.—You mean, *now?* (*Empties ashtray on coffee table to waste can under bar.*) Well, Alan, ole boy, it's a friend's birthday and I'm having a few people.—No, you wouldn't exactly call it a birthday party—well, yes, actually I guess you would. I mean, what else would you call it? A *wake,* maybe. (*Ashtray back to coffee table.*) I'm sorry I can't ask you to join us—but—well, kiddo, it just wouldn't work out.—No, it's not place cards or anything. It's just that—well, I'd hate to just see you for ten minutes and . . . Alan? Alan? What's the matter?—Are you—are you crying?—Oh, Alan, what's wrong?—Alan, listen, come on over. No, no, it's perfectly all right. Well, just hurry up. I mean, come on by and have a drink, okay? Alan . . . are you all right? Okay. Yeah. Same old address. Yeah. Bye. (*He sits on stool and slowly hangs up, stares blankly into space.*)

(DONALD *appears, bathed and changed. He strikes a pose on landing.*)

DONALD. Well. Am I stunning?

MICHAEL. (*He looks up. Tonelessly.*) You're absolutely stunning.—You look like shit, but I'm absolutely stunned.

DONALD. (*Crestfallen, goes to bar.*) Your grapes are, how you say, sour.

MICHAEL. Listen, you won't believe what just happened.

DONALD. Where's my drink?

MICHAEL. I didn't make it— I've been on the phone. (DONALD *makes himself a martini.*) My old roommate from Georgetown just called.

DONALD. Alan what's-his-name?

MICHAEL. McCarthy. He's up here from Washington on business or something and he's on his way over here.

DONALD. Well I hope he knows the lyrics to Happy Birthday.

MICHAEL. (*Rises with phone.*) Listen, asshole, what am I going to do? He's *straight*. And *Square City! ("Top Drawer" accent through clenched teeth.*) I mean he's rally vury proper. Auffully good family.

DONALD. (*Same accent.*) That's *so* important.

MICHAEL. (*Regular speech.*) I mean his family looks down on people in the theatre—so whatta you think he'll feel about the freak show we've got booked for dinner? (*Returns phone to desk and crosses to Left end of sofa.*)

DONALD. (*Sipping his drink.*) Christ, is that good. (*Sits in Down Right chair.*)

MICHAEL. Want some cracked crab?

DONALD. Not just yet. Why'd you invite him over?

MICHAEL. I didn't. He invited himself. He said he had to see me tonight. Immediately. He absolutely lost his spring on the phone—started crying. (*Crosses to DONALD.*)

DONALD. Maybe he's feeling sorry for himself too.

MICHAEL. Great heaves and sobs. Really boo-hoo-hoo-time—and that's not his style at all. I mean he's so pulled-together he wouldn't show any emotion if he were in a plane crash. What am I going to do? (*Gets a glass and ice at bar.*)

DONALD. What the hell do you care what he thinks?

MICHAEL. Well, I don't really.

DONALD. Or are you suddenly ashamed of your friends?

MICHAEL. Donald, *you* are the only person I know of whom I am truly ashamed. Some people *do* have different standards from yours and mine, you know. And if we don't acknowledge them, we're just as narrow-minded and backward as we think they are.

DONALD. You know what you are, Michael? You're a *real* person.

MICHAEL. Thank you and fuck you. (MICHAEL *points to crab.*) Want some?

DONALD. No, thanks. (MICHAEL *crosses to bar and opens club soda.*) How could you ever have been friends with a bore like that?

MICHAEL. Believe it or not there was a time in my life when I didn't go around *announcing* that I was a faggot.

DONALD. That must have been before speech replaced sign language. (*Goes to other side of ottoman.*)

MICHAEL. (*Crosses to Right end of sofa with glass.*) Don't give me any static on that score. I didn't come out until I left college.

DONALD. It seems to me that the first time we tricked we met in a gay bar on Third Avenue during your junior year.

MICHAEL. Cunt.

DONALD. I thought you'd never say it.

MICHAEL. Sure you don't want any cracked crab?

DONALD. *Not yet! If you don't mind!*

MICHAEL. Well, it can only be getting colder. (*Puts glass on coffee table and picks up crab and leaves it on Left table.*) What time is it?

DONALD. I don't know. Early. (*Goes to bar.*)

MICHAEL. Where the hell is Alan? (*Goes to coffee table for glass.*)

DONALD. Do you want some more club soda? (*Picking up soda bottle.*)

MICHAEL. What?

DONALD. There's nothing but club soda in that glass. It's not gin—like mine. You want some more?

MICHAEL. No. (*Puts glass on coffee table and goes to desk for cigarettes.*)

DONALD. I've been watching you for several Saturdays now. You've actually stopped drinking, haven't you?

MICHAEL. And smoking too. (*Opening cigarettes at Up Left end of sofa.*)

DONALD. And smoking too. How long's it been?

MICHAEL. Five weeks.

DONALD. That's amazing.

MICHAEL. I've found God. (*Goes to waste can with wrappings.*)

DONALD. (*Crosses above sofa to ottoman.*) It is amazing—for you.

MICHAEL. Or is God dead?

DONALD. (*Sits on ottoman.*) Yes, thank God. And don't get panicky just because I'm paying you a compliment. I can tell the difference.

MICHAEL. (*Crosses to Right end coffee table.*) You always said that I held my liquor better than anybody you ever saw.

DONALD. I could always tell when you were getting high —one way.

MICHAEL. I'd get hostile.

DONALD. You seem happier or something now—and that shows.

MICHAEL. (*Quietly.*) Thanks. (*Puts opened cigarettes on coffee table and exits to kitchen for beer tub.*)

DONALD. What made you stop—the analyst?

MICHAEL. (*Offstage.*) He certainly had a lot to do with it. (*Returns from kitchen and puts beer tub under bar.*) Mainly, I just didn't think I could survive another hangover, that's all. I don't think I could get through that morning-after ick attack.

DONALD. Morning-after what?

MICHAEL. Icks! Anxiety! Guilt! Unfathomable guilt—either real or imagined—from that split second your eyes pop open and you say, "Oh, my God, what did I do last night!" and ZAP, Total Recall! (*Picks up two ashtrays from bar.*)

DONALD. *Tell* me about it!

MICHAEL. (*Goes to Left table leaving an ashtray.*) Then, the coffee, aspirin, alka-seltzer, darvon, deprisal, and a quick call to I.A.—Ick's Anonymous.

DONALD. "Good morning, I.A."

MICHAEL. (*Crosses in.*) "Hi! Was I too bad last night? Did I do anything wrong? I didn't do anything terrible, did I?"

DONALD. (*Laughing.*) How many times! How many times!

MICHAEL. (*Takes ashtray to desk.*) And from then on, that struggle to live til lunch when you have a double Bloody Mary—that is, if you've *waited* until lunch—and then you're half-pissed again and useless for the rest of the afternoon. And the only sure cure is to go to bed for about thirty-seven hours but who ever does that. Instead, you hang on til cocktail time, and by then you're ready for what the night holds—which hopefully is another party where the whole goddam cycle starts over! (*Crosses to Right end of coffee table.*) Well, I've been on that merry-go-round long enough and I either had to get off or die of centrifugal force.

DONALD. And just how does a clear head *stack up* with the dull fog of alcohol?

MICHAEL. Well, all those things you've always heard are true. Nothing can compare with the experience of one's faculties functioning at their maximum natural capacity. The only thing is . . . I'd *kill* for a drink.

(*The BUZZER sounds.*)

DONALD. Joe College has finally arrived.

MICHAEL. (*He puts his drink on coffee table and goes to door and presses the wall panel button.*) Suddenly, I have such an ick! (*Crosses back to* DONALD.) Now listen, Donald . . .

DONALD. (*Rises. Quick.*) Michael, don't insult me by giving me any lecture on acceptable social behavior. I promise to sit with my legs spread apart and keep my voice in a deep register.

MICHAEL. Donald, you are a real *card-carrying cunt.*

(*The apartment door BUZZES.* MICHAEL *goes to door and opens it and* DONALD *goes to base of steps.*)

EMORY. (*Offstage.*) ALL RIGHT THIS IS A RAID! EVERYBODY'S UNDER ARREST! (EMORY *is in Bermuda shorts and a sweater. He enters and gives* MICHAEL *a kiss on the cheek, refers to dish:* EMORY *carries a covered dish.*) Hello, darlin'! Connie Casserole. Oh, Mary, don't ask.

MICHAEL. Hello, Emory. Put it in the kitchen.

(EMORY *spots* DONALD *and goes to him.*)

EMORY. Who is this exotic woman over here?

(HANK *enters first, then* LARRY. LARRY *has on a shirt and pants.* HANK *is in a suit and tie.* LARRY *and* HANK *carry birthday gifts.*)

MICHAEL. Hi, Hank. Larry.

(*They say, "Hi," shake hands, enter.* HANK *crosses to Right end of coffee table and* LARRY *goes above sofa.* MICHAEL *looks out in the hall, comes back into the room, closes the door.*)

DONALD. Hi, Emory.

EMORY. My dear, I thought you had perished! Where have you been hiding your classically chiseled features?

DONALD. (*To* EMORY.) I don't live in the city any more.

MICHAEL. (*To* LARRY *and* HANK *re: the gifts.*) Here, I'll take those. Where's yours, Emory?

EMORY. It's arriving later. (EMORY *exits to the kitchen.*)

(LARRY *and* DONALD'S *eyes have met.* HANK *has handed* MICHAEL *his gift.* LARRY *is too preoccupied.*)

HANK. Larry! Larry!

LARRY. What!

HANK. Give Michael the gift!

LARRY. Oh. Here. (LARRY *crosses, gives gift to* MICHAEL *who puts box on third step and leans poster against step pillar. To* HANK.) Louder. So my mother in Philadelphia can hear you.

HANK. Well, you were just standing there in a trance.

MICHAEL. (*To* LARRY *and* HANK.) You both know Donald, don't you?

DONALD. Sure. Nice to see you. (*To* HANK.) Hi.

HANK. (*Shaking hands.*) Nice to meet you. (*Continues crosses to Down Left chair.*)

MICHAEL. Oh, I thought you'd met.

DONALD. Well . . .

LARRY. We haven't exactly met but we've . . . Hi. (*Crosses to* HANK.)

DONALD. Hi. (*Crosses and sits Down Right chair.*)

HANK. But you've what?

LARRY. . . . Seen . . . each other before.

MICHAEL. Well, *that* sounds murky.

(EMORY *re-enters from kitchen crossing to* MICHAEL *at Center.*)

HANK. You've never met but you've seen each other.

LARRY. What was wrong with the way *I* said it.

HANK. Where?

EMORY. (*Loud aside to* MICHAEL.) I think they're going to have their first fight.

LARRY. (*Leans on landing.*) The first one since we got out of the taxi.

MICHAEL. (*Re:* EMORY.) Where'd you find this trash?

LARRY. Downstairs leaning against a lamppost.

EMORY. With an orchid behind my ear and big wet lips painted over the lipline.

MICHAEL. Just like Maria Montez.

DONALD. Oh, *please!*

EMORY. (*Crossing to* DONALD.) What have you got against Maria?—she was a good woman. (*Crosses above sofa.*)

MICHAEL. Listen, everybody, this old college friend of mine is in town and he's stopping by for a fast drink on his way to dinner somewhere. But, listen, he's *straight.* (*Crosses to* EMORY.)

LARRY. *Straight!* If it's the one I met he's about as straight as the Yellow Brick Road.

MICHAEL. (*Crosses in.*) No, you met Justin Stuart.

(EMORY *exits kitchen Up Center.*)

HANK. I don't remember meeting anybody named Justin Stuart.

LARRY. Of course you don't, dope. *I* met him.

MICHAEL. Well, this is someone else.

DONALD. Alan McCarthy. A very close total stranger.

MICHAEL. It's not that I care what he would think of me, really—it's just that *he's* not ready for it. And he never will be. You understand that, don't you, Hank?

(EMORY *enters Up Center and crosses to landing.*)

HANK. Oh, sure.

LARRY. You honestly think he doesn't know about you?

MICHAEL. If there's the slightest suspicion, he's never let-on one bit.

EMORY. What's he had, a lobotomy? (*He continues to bath for a Kleenex picking up the vicuna sweater from floor enroute and putting it on the bed.*)

MICHAEL. I was super careful when I was in college and I still am whenever I see him. I don't know why, but I am.

DONALD. Tilt.

MICHAEL. (*Crosses to Center.*) You may think it was a crock of shit, Donald, but to him I'm sure we were close friends. The closest. To pop that balloon now just wouldn't be fair to him. Isn't that right? (*Looks to LARRY.*)

LARRY. Whatever's fair.

(LARRY *gives* HANK *a look and* HANK *goes around staircase looking over apartment, ending up at Center.*)

MICHAEL. Well, of course. And if that's phony of me, Donald, then that's phony of me and make something of it.

DONALD. I pass.

MICHAEL. (*Crosses to* DONALD.) Well, even you have to admit it's much simpler to deal with the world according to its rules and then go right ahead and do what you damn well please. You do understand *that*, don't you?

DONALD. Now that you've put it in layman's terms.

MICHAEL. I was just like Alan when I was in college. Very large in the dating department. Wore nothing but those constipated Ivy League clothes and those ten-pound cordovan shoes. (*To* HANK.) No offense.

HANK. Quite all right. (*Goes to bar.*)

(EMORY *enters from bath and comes down steps.*)

MICHAEL. I butched-it-up quite a bit. And I didn't think I was lying to myself. I really thought I was straight. (*Goes to steps.*)

EMORY. Who do you have to fuck to get a drink around here? (*Stops on steps.*)

MICHAEL. Will you light somewhere? (EMORY *sits on steps.*) Or I thought I thought I was straight. I know I didn't come out til after I'd graduated.

DONALD. What about all those week ends up from school?

MICHAEL. (*Crosses in.*) I still wasn't out. I was still in the "Christ-Was-I-Drunk-Last-Night Syndrome."

LARRY. The *what?*

MICHAEL. (*Crosses Center.*) The Christ-Was-I-Drunk-Last-Night Syndrome. You know, when you made it with some guy in school and the next day when you had to face each other there was always a lot of shit-kicking crap about, "Man, was I drunk last night! Christ, I don't remember a thing!"

DONALD. You were just guilty because you were Catholic, that's all.

MICHAEL. (*Crosses to Left end coffee table.*) That's not true. The Christ-Was-I-Drunk-Last-Night Syndrome knows no religion. It has to do with immaturity. Although I will admit there's a high percentage of it among Mormons.

EMORY. Trollop.

MICHAEL. (*Crosses to Left table.*) Somehow, we all managed to justify our actions in those days. I later found out that even Justin Stuart, my closest friend—

DONALD. Other than Alan McCarthy.

MICHAEL. (*A look to* DONALD.) —was doing the same thing. Only Justin was going to Boston on week ends.

LARRY. (*To* HANK.) Sound familiar? (*Crosses to* HANK, *motions* HANK *to give him the cigarettes.*)

MICHAEL. (*Takes crab to coffee table.*) Yes, long before Justin or I or God-only-knows how many others *came out,* we used to get drunk and "horse-around" a bit. You see, in the Christ-Was-I-Drunk-Last-Night Syndrome, you really *are* drunk. That part of it is true. It's just that you also *do remember everything.* Oh God, I use to have to get loaded to go in a gay bar!

DONALD. Well, times certainly have changed.

MICHAEL. They *have*. Lately I've gotten to despise the bars. Everybody just standing around and standing around —it's like one eternal intermission.

HANK. (*To* LARRY.) Sound familiar?

EMORY. I can't stand the bars either. All that cat-and-mouse business—you hang around *staring* at each other all night and wind-up going home alone.

MICHAEL. And pissed.

LARRY. (*Goes to sofa.*) A lot of guys have to get loaded to have sex. (*Quick look to* HANK *who is unamused.*) So I've been told. (*Sits sofa, Right end.*)

MICHAEL. (*Crosses to* DONALD.) If you remember, Donald, the first time we made it I was so drunk I could hardly stand up.

DONALD. You were so drunk you could hardly get-it-up.

MICHAEL. (*Mock innocence.*) Christ, I was so drunk I don't remember.

DONALD. Bullshit, you remember.

MICHAEL. (*Sings to* DONALD.) "Just friends, lovers no more . . ."

EMORY. You may as well be. Everybody thinks you are anyway.

DONALD. We never *were—really*.

MICHAEL. We didn't have time to be—we got to know each other too fast. (*The door BUZZER sounds.*) Oh, Jesus, it's Alan! (LARRY, HANK, *and* DONALD *uncross their legs.*) Now, please everybody, do me a favor and cool-it for the few minutes he's here. (*Goes to door and pushes panel button.*)

EMORY. (*Rises and goes to Left end sofa.*) Anything for a sis, Mary.

MICHAEL. (*Crosses to* EMORY.) That's *exactly* what I'm talking about, Emory. *No camping!*

EMORY. Sorry. (*Sits Left end sofa. Deep, deep voice to* DONALD.) Think the Giants are gonna win the pennant this year?

DONALD. (*Deep, deep voice.*) Fuckin' A, Mac. (*Rises and goes to Left of steps.*)

(MICHAEL *goes to the door, opens it to reveal* BERNARD, *dressed in a shirt and tie and a Brooks Brothers jacket. He carries a birthday gift and two bottles of red wine.*)

EMORY. (*Big scream.*) Oh, it's only another queen!
BERNARD. And it ain't the Red one, either.
EMORY. It's the queen of spades!

(BERNARD *enters.* MICHAEL *looks out in the hall.*)

MICHAEL. Bernard, is the downstairs door open? (*Closing door.*)
BERNARD. It was, but I closed it.
MICHAEL. Good. (BERNARD *starts to put wine on bar. Re: the two bottles of red wine.*) I'll take those. You can put your present with the others.

(BERNARD *hands him the wine. The PHONE rings.*)

BERNARD. Hi, Larry. Hi, Hank. (*Crossing below coffee table to steps.*)
MICHAEL. *Christ of the Andes!* Donald, will you bartend, please?

(MICHAEL *gives* DONALD *the wine bottles, goes to the phone.* DONALD *puts wine on Left table as* BERNARD *puts gift on steps.*)

BERNARD. Hello, Donald. Good to see you.
MICHAEL. (*Into phone.*) Hello?
DONALD. Bernard.
MICHAEL. Alan?
EMORY. Hi, Bernardette. Anybody ever tell you you'd look divine in a hammock, surrounded by louvres and ceiling fans and lots and lots of lush tropical ferns?
BERNARD. (*To* EMORY.) You're *such* a fag. You take the cake.

(BERNARD *and* DONALD *ad-lib Left of steps.*)

EMORY. Oh, what *about* the cake—whose job was that?

LARRY. Mine. I ordered one to be delivered.

EMORY. How many candles did you say put on it—eighty?

MICHAEL. . . . What? Wait a minute. There's too much noise. Let me go to another phone. (*He presses the hold button, hangs up, dashes toward stairs.*)

LARRY. (*Rises and goes above sofa.*) Michael, did the cake come?

MICHAEL. No.

DONALD. (*To* MICHAEL.) What's up?

MICHAEL. Do I know?

LARRY. Jesus, I'd better call. Okay if I use the private line?

MICHAEL. (*Going upstairs.*) Sure. Go ahead. (*Stops dead on stairs, turns.*) Listen, everybody, there's some cracked crab there. Help yourselves.

(DONALD *shakes his head.* MICHAEL *continues up the stairs to the bedroom.* LARRY *crosses to the phone, presses the free line button, picks up receiver, dials Information.* HANK *rises and sits Right end sofa for crab.*)

DONALD. Is everybody ready for a drink? (*Goes to bar.*)

EMORY. (*Flipping up his sweater and rising.*) *Ready!* I'll be your topless cocktail waitress.

BERNARD. Please spare us the sight of your sagging tits.

EMORY. (*To* HANK, LARRY.) What're you having, kids?

MICHAEL. (*Having picked up the bedside phone.*) Yes, Alan . . .

LARRY. Vodka and tonic. (*Into phone.*) Could I have the number for the Marseilles Bakery in Manhattan.

EMORY. (*Crosses to* HANK *above sofa.*) A vod and ton and a . . .

HANK. Is there any beer?

EMORY. Beer! Who drinks beer before dinner?

BERNARD. Beer drinkers.

DONALD. That's telling him.

MICHAEL. . . . No, Alan, don't be silly. What's there to apologize for?

EMORY. Truck drivers do. Or . . . or wall-paperers. Not school teachers. They have sherry.

HANK. This one has beer.

EMORY. Well, maybe school teachers in public schools. (*To* LARRY.) How can a sensitive artist like you live with an insensitive bull like that?

LARRY. (*Hanging up the phone and re-dialing.*) I can't.

BERNARD. Emory, you'd live with Hank in a minute, if he'd ask you. In fifty-eight seconds. Lord knows, you're *sss*ensitive.

EMORY. (*Crosses to Center.*) Why don't you have a piece of watermelon and hush-up!

MICHAEL. . . . Alan, don't be ridiculous.

DONALD. (*Giving beer can to* HANK.) Here you go, Hank.

HANK. Thanks.

LARRY. Shit. They don't answer.

DONALD. (*Handing* BERNARD'S *beer to* EMORY *who takes it to* BERNARD.) What're you having, Emory?

BERNARD. A Pink Lady.

EMORY. A vodka martini on-the-rocks, please. (*Slaps* BERNARD'S *outstretched hand, hands him the beer and goes to Left table, looks at wine.*)

LARRY. (*Hangs up.*) Well, let's just hope.

(DONALD *hands* LARRY *his drink.* DONALD *returns to the bar to make* EMORY'S *drink.* LARRY *sit on steps and* BERNARD *goes above sofa.*)

MICHAEL. Lunch tomorrow will be great. One o'clock—the Oak Room at the Plaza okay? Fine.

BERNARD. (*To* DONALD.) Donald, read any new libraries lately?

DONALD. One or three. I did the complete works of Doris Lessing this week. I've been depressed.

MICHAEL. Alan, forget it, will you? Bye, bye. (MICHAEL *hangs up.*)

DONALD. You must not work in Circulation any more.

BERNARD. Oh, I'm still there—every day.

DONALD. Well, since I moved, I only come in on Saturday evenings. (DONALD *moves his stack of books off the bar and goes to making a pitcher of vodka martinis.*)

HANK. Looks like you stock-up for the week.

(MICHAEL *crosses to steps landing.*)

BERNARD. Are you kidding?—that'll last him two days.

EMORY. It would last *me* two years. I still haven't finished "Atlas Shrugged" which I started in 1912.

MICHAEL. (*To* DONALD.) Well, he's not coming.

DONALD. It's just as well now.

BERNARD. Some people eat, some people drink, and some take dope.

DONALD. I read.

MICHAEL. And read and read and read. It's a wonder your eyes don't turn back in your head at the sight of a dust jacket.

HANK. Well, at least, he's a constructive escapist.

MICHAEL. Yeah, what do I do?—take planes. No, I don't do that any more. Because I don't have the *money* to do that any more. I go to the baths. That's about it.

EMORY. I'm about to do both. I'm flying to the West Coast—

BERNARD. You still have that act with a donkey in Tijuana?

(MICHAEL *decides on change of sweater. Goes to bedroom for a red one.*)

EMORY. (*Crosses to* BERNARD.) I'm going to San Francisco on a well-earned vacation.

LARRY. No shopping?

EMORY. (*Sits Left end sofa.*) Oh, I'll look for a few things for a couple of clients but I've been so busy lately, I really couldn't care less if I never saw another piece of fabric or another stick of furniture as long as I live. I'm going to the Club Baths and I'm not coming out til they announce the departure of TWA one week later.

(DONALD *pours* EMORY *a glass and refills his glass from pitcher.*)

BERNARD. (*To* EMORY.) You'll never learn to stay out of the baths, will you. (*Crosses Center to* LARRY.) The last time Emily was taking the vapors, this big hairy number strolled in. Emory said, "I'm just resting," and the big hairy number said, "I'm just *ar*resting!" It was the vice! (*Goes to Down Right chair.*)

EMORY. You have to tell everything, don't you.

DONALD. (*Crosses to give* EMORY *his drink.*) Here you go, Emory.

EMORY. Thanks, sonny. You live with your parents?

DONALD. Yeah. But it's all right—they're gay. (EMORY *roars, slaps* HANK *on the knee.* HANK *gets up, moves away to phonograph. To* MICHAEL.) What happened to Alan?

MICHAEL. He suddenly got terrible icks about having broken down on the phone. Kept apologizing over and over. Did a big about-face and reverted to the old Alan right before my very eyes.

DONALD. Ears.

MICHAEL. Ears. Well, the cracked crab obviously did not work out. (*He starts to take away the tray on coffee table.*)

EMORY. Just put that down if you don't want your hand slapped. I'm about to have some.

MICHAEL. It's really very good. (*Gives* DONALD *a look.*) I don't know why everyone has such an aversion to it. (*Picking up his glass from coffee table.*)

DONALD. Sometimes you remind me of the Chinese water torture. I take that back. Sometimes you remind me

of the *relentless* Chinese water torture. (*Sits on high stool
with his drink.*)

MICHAEL. Bitch. (*Goes to bar to refill glass.*)

(HANK *has put on some MUSIC.*)

BERNARD. Yeah, baby, let's hear that sound.

EMORY. A drum beat and their eyes sparkle like
Cartier's.

(BERNARD *starts to snap his fingers and move in time
with the music.*)

HANK. (*Crosses in above sofa.*) Michael, I wonder
where Harold is?

EMORY. Yeah, where *is* the frozen fruit?

MICHAEL. (*To* DONALD.) Emory refers to Harold as
the frozen fruit because of his former profession as an ice
skater.

EMORY. She used to be the Vera Hruba Ralston of the
Borscht Circuit. ice skater turned more ounss

(MICHAEL *and* BERNARD *dance.* LARRY *is dancing alone.*
HANK *goes to* LARRY *but doesn't dance and* HANK
goes back to desk.)

BERNARD. (*To* MICHAEL.) If your mother could see you
now she'd have a stroke.

MICHAEL. Got a camera on you?

LARRY. Let's go, Miss Montez!

(EMORY *goes to* LARRY *to dance. As* EMORY *gets to* LARRY
the door BUZZER sounds.)

EMORY. (*Lets out a yelp.*) Oh my God, it's Lilly Law!
Everybody three feet apart!

(MICHAEL *goes to the panel button and presses it and*

opens the door and looks out. HANK *turns off the PHONOGRAPH.* EMORY *quickly sits on sofa.* BERNARD *quickly sits in Down Right chair.* LARRY *quickly sits on steps.*)

BERNARD. It's probably Harold now.

MICHAEL. (*He leans back in the room.*) No, it's the delivery boy from the bakery.

LARRY. Thank God.

(MICHAEL *goes out into the hall,* HANK *goes to door and looks out.*)

EMORY. (*Loudly.*) Ask him if he's got any hot cross buns!

HANK. (*Crosses to* EMORY.) Come on, Emory, knock it off.

BERNARD. You can take her anywhere but out.

EMORY. (*To* HANK.) You remind me of an old maid school teacher.

HANK. You remind me of a chicken wing. (*Goes to phonograph.*)

EMORY. I'm sure you meant that as a compliment.

(HANK *turns the MUSIC on.*)

MICHAEL. (*In hall.*) Thank you, good night. (MICHAEL *returns with a cake box, closes the door, and takes it into the kitchen.*)

LARRY. (*Goes to Left table.*) Hey, Bernard, you remember that thing we used to do on Fire Island? (LARRY *starts to do a kind of "Madison."*)

BERNARD. (*Rises and crosses in.*) That was "in" so far back I think I've forgotten.

EMORY. *I* remember.

(*Goes to* LARRY *and starts doing the steps.* LARRY *and* BERNARD *start to follow.* BERNARD *crosses to* EMORY.)

LARRY. Well, show us.

MICHAEL. (*He enters from the kitchen, falls in line with them.*) Well, if it isn't the Geriatrics Rockettes. (*Now* ALL *are doing practically a precision routine.* DONALD *comes to above sofa, sips his drink, and watches in fascination.* HANK *goes to sofa and sits. At a point in the dance the door BUZZER sounds. No one seems to hear it.* HANK *turns toward the door, hesitates. He looks toward* MICHAEL *who is now deeply involved in the intricacies of the dance. No one, it seems, has heard it but* HANK. *He goes to the door, opens it wide to reveal* ALAN. *He is dressed in black-tie. The* DANCERS *continue, turning and slapping their knees and heels and laughing with abandon as* ALAN *goes to Right end of coffee table. Suddenly,* MICHAEL *looks up, stops dead.* HANK *goes to the RECORD PLAYER, turns it off abruptly.* EMORY, LARRY, *and* BERNARD *scatter as though they were not dancing.* BERNARD *walks out of dance up steps.* LARRY *goes around step unit and* EMORY *sits in Down Left chair. At otto-man.*) I thought you said you weren't coming.

(BERNARD *returns down steps and sits on third step.* LARRY *returns to Left table area and gets his drink.*)

ALAN. I . . . well, I'm sorry . . .

MICHAEL. (*Forced lightly.*) We were just—acting silly . . .

ALAN. Actually, when I called I was in a phone booth around the corner. My dinner party is not far from here. And . . .

MICHAEL. Emory was just showing us this . . . silly dance.

ALAN. . . . well, then I walked past and your downstairs door was open and . . .

MICHAEL. This is Emory. (EMORY *curtsies and sits on steps between* BERNARD'S *legs.* MICHAEL *glares at him.* HANK *closes door and goes to Down Right chair.*) Everybody, this is Alan McCarthy. Counterclockwise, Alan: Larry, Emory, Bernard, Donald, and Hank.

(ALL *mumble "Hello," "Hi," and* LARRY *moves in to
    steps near* EMORY *and* BERNARD *as introduced.*)

HANK. Nice to meet you.
ALAN. Good to meet you. (*Shaking hands with* HANK.)
MICHAEL. Would you like a drink?
ALAN. Thanks, no. I . . . I can't stay . . . long . . .
really.
MICHAEL. Well, you're here now, so stay. What would
you like?
ALAN. Do you have any rye?
MICHAEL. I'm afraid I don't drink it any more. You'll
have to settle for gin or scotch or vodka.
DONALD. Or beer.
ALAN. Scotch, please.

(MICHAEL *starts for bar.*)

DONALD. I'll get it. (*Goes to bar.*)
HANK. Guess I'm the only beer drinker.
ALAN. (*Looking around* GROUP.) Whose . . . birthday
. . . is it?
LARRY. Harold's.
ALAN. (*Looking from face to face.*) Harold?
BERNARD. He's not here yet.
EMORY. She's never been on time— (BERNARD *nudges*
EMORY *with his knee.* MICHAEL *shoots* EMORY *a wither-
ing glance.*) He's never been on time in his—
MICHAEL. (*Crosses to* ALAN.) Alan's from Washington.
We went to college together. Georgetown.
EMORY. Well, isn't that fascinating?
DONALD. (*He hands* ALAN *his drink.*) If that's too
strong, I'll put some water in it.
ALAN. It looks fine. Thanks.

(DONALD *goes to desk.*)

HANK. Are you in the government?

ALAN. No. I'm a lawyer. What . . . what do you do?

HANK. I teach school.

ALAN. Oh. I would have taken you for an athlete of some sort. You look like you might play sports . . . of some sort.

HANK. Well, I'm no professional but I was on the basketball team in college and I play quite a bit of tennis.

ALAN. I play tennis too.

HANK. Great game.

ALAN. Yes. Great. (*A beat. Silence as* LARRY, BERNARD *and* EMORY *look bored.*) What . . . do you teach?

HANK. Math.

ALAN. Math?

HANK. Yes.

ALAN. Math. Well.

EMORY. Kinda makes you want to rush out and buy a slide rule, doesn't it?

MICHAEL. (*Pulling* EMORY *to his feet.*) Emory. I'm going to need some help with dinner and you're elected.

EMORY. I'm *always* elected.

BERNARD. You're a natural born domestic.

★ EMORY. Said the African queen! You come on too—you can fan me while I make the salad dressing.

MICHAEL. (*Glaring: phony smile.*) RIGHT THIS WAY, EMORY! (MICHAEL *pushes* EMORY *and* BERNARD *to kitchen. They exit and he follows. The muffled sound of* MICHAEL'S *voice can be heard.*) You son-of-a-bitch!

EMORY. (*Offstage.*) What the hell do you want from me?

HANK. Why don't we all sit down? (*Sits Left end sofa.*)

ALAN. Sure. (*Sits Right end of sofa.*)

(HANK *and* ALAN *come to sit on the couch.* LARRY *at steps as* DONALD *goes to steps and sits on third step.*)

LARRY. Hi.

DONALD. Hi.

ALAN. I really feel terrible—barging in on you fellows this way.

LARRY. (*To* DONALD.) How've you been?

DONALD. Fine, thanks.

HANK. (*To* ALAN.) Oh, that's okay.

DONALD. (*To* LARRY.) And you?

LARRY. Oh . . . just fine.

ALAN. (*To* HANK.) You're married?

(MICHAEL *enters from the kitchen.*)

HANK. What?

ALAN. I see you're married. (*He points to* HANK'S *wedding band.*)

HANK. Oh.

MICHAEL. Yes. Hank's married.

ALAN. You have any kids?

HANK. Yes. Two. A boy nine, and a girl seven. You should see my boy play tennis—really puts his dad to shame. (HANK *looks toward* DONALD.)

DONALD. I better get some ice. (*He exits to kitchen with ice bucket.*)

ALAN. (*To* HANK.) I have two kids too. Both girls.

HANK. Great.

MICHAEL. How *are* the girls, Alan? (*Sits ottoman.*)

ALAN. Oh, just sensational. (*Shakes his head.*) They're something, those kids. God, I'm nuts about them.

HANK. How long have you been married?

ALAN. Nine years. Can you believe it, Mickey?

MICHAEL. No.

ALAN. Mickey used to go with my wife when we were all in school.

MICHAEL. Can you believe that?

ALAN. (*To* HANK.) You live in the city?

LARRY. Yes, we do. (LARRY *comes over to couch next to* HANK.)

ALAN. Oh.

HANK. I'm in the process of getting a divorce. Larry and I are—roommates.

MICHAEL. Yes.

ALAN. Oh. I'm sorry. Oh, I mean—

HANK. I understand.

ALAN. (*Gets up.*) I . . . I . . . I think I'd like another drink . . . if I may.

MICHAEL. (*Rises.*) Of course. What was it?

ALAN. I'll do it . . . if I may. (*He goes to the bar. Suddenly, there is a loud Offstage CRASH. ALAN jumps, looks toward kitchen.*) What was that?

(DONALD *enters with the ice bucket.*)

MICHAEL. Excuse me. Testy temperament out in the kitch!

(MICHAEL *exits Up Center to kitchen.* ALAN *continues nervously picking-up and putting-down bottles, searching for the scotch.*)

HANK. (*To* LARRY.) Larry, where do you know that guy from?

LARRY. What guy?

(DONALD *is crossing below coffee table with ice bucket to above* ALAN *at the bar.*)

HANK. *That* guy.

LARRY. I don't know. Around. The bars. (*Goes to Left table.*)

DONALD. Can I help you, Alan?

ALAN. I . . . I can't seem to find the scotch.

DONALD. You've got it in your hand.

ALAN. Oh. Of course. How . . . stupid of me.

(DONALD *watches* ALAN *fumble with the scotch bottle and glass.*)

DONALD. Why don't you let me do that?

ALAN. (*Gratefully hands him both.*) Thanks.

DONALD. Was it water or soda?
ALAN. Just make it straight—over ice.

(MICHAEL *enters crossing to Left end sofa.*)

MICHAEL. You see, Alan, I told you it wasn't a good
time to talk. But we—
ALAN. (*At Right end of sofa.*) It doesn't matter. I'll
just finish this and go. (DONALD *gives* ALAN *his drink.
He takes a long swallow.*)
LARRY. (*Crosses to ottoman and sits.*) Where can
Harold be?
MICHAEL. Oh, he's always late. You know how neurotic
he is about going out in public. It takes him hours to get
ready.
LARRY. Why *is* that?

(EMORY *breezes in via above steps from kitchen, carrying
a stack of plates which he places on Left table and
picks up two wine bottles.*)

EMORY. Why is what?
LARRY. Why does Harold spend hours getting ready before he can go out?
EMORY. Because she's a sick lady, that's why. (*Exits
kitchen via Up Center with two wine bottles.*)

(ALAN *finishes his drink.*)

MICHAEL. Alan, as I was about to say, we can go in the
bedroom and talk.
ALAN. It really doesn't matter.
MICHAEL. Come on. Bring your drink.
ALAN. I . . . I've finished it.
MICHAEL. Well, make another and come on.

(DONALD *picks up the scotch bottle and pours into the
glass* ALAN *has in his hand.* MICHAEL *has started for
the stairs.*)

ALAN. (*To* DONALD.) Thanks.

DONALD. Don't mention it. (*Picks up club soda bottle and exits kitchen.*)

ALAN. (*To* HANK.) Excuse us. We'll be down in a minute. (*Goes to steps.*)

HANK. Sure. Sure.

LARRY. Oh, he'll still be here.

(*Rises and crosses to bar leaving glass at bar.* ALAN *turns at bottom of steps and* MICHAEL *indicates steps.*)

MICHAEL. This way, Alan.

(ALAN *and* MICHAEL *linger on landing a bit looking out window.*)

HANK. (*To* LARRY.) What was *that* supposed to mean?

LARRY. What was what supposed to mean?

HANK. You know.

LARRY. You want another beer?

HANK. No. You're jealous, aren't you?

(HANK *starts to laugh.* LARRY *doesn't like it.* DONALD *enters from kitchen via Upstage of stairs with his drink.* ALAN *and* MICHAEL *go to bedroom.*)

LARRY. I'm Larry— *You're* jealous. (*Crosses to* DONALD.) Hey, Donald, where've you been hanging out these days? I haven't seen you in a long time.

(LARRY *sits on steps with* DONALD *standing in front of* LARRY *talking quietly.* HANK *exits into the kitchen.*)

ALAN. (*To* MICHAEL.) This is a marvelous apartment.

MICHAEL. It's too expensive. I work to pay rent.

ALAN. What are you doing these days?

MICHAEL. Nothing.

ALAN. Aren't you writing any more?

MICHAEL. I haven't looked at a typewriter since I sold the very very wonderful, very very marvelous *screenplay* which never got produced.

ALAN. (*Crosses to* MICHAEL.) That's right, the last time I saw you, you were on your way to California. Or was it Europe?

MICHAEL. Hollywood. Which is not in Europe nor does it have anything whatsoever to do with California.

ALAN. (*Crosses to pillar.*) I've never been there but I would imagine it's awful. Everyone must be terribly cheap.

MICHAEL. No, not everyone. Alan, I want to try to explain this evening . . .

ALAN. What's there to explain? (*Crosses to chair.*) Sometimes you just can't invite everybody to every party and some people take it personally. But I'm not one of them. I should apologize for inviting myself.

MICHAEL. (*Sits bench.*) That's not exactly what I meant.

ALAN. Your friends all seem like very nice guys. That Hank is really a very attractive fellow.

MICHAEL. . . . Yes. He is.

ALAN. We have a lot in common. What's his roommate's name?

MICHAEL. Larry.

ALAN. . . . What does *he* do?

MICHAEL. He's a commercial artist.

ALAN. I liked Donald too. The only one I didn't care too much for was—what's his name—Emory?

MICHAEL. Yes. Emory.

ALAN. (*Puts drink on Upstage table.*) I just can't stand that kind of talk. It just grates on me.

MICHAEL. What kind of talk, Alan?

ALAN. (*Crosses to* MICHAEL.) Oh, you know. His brand of humor, I guess.

MICHAEL. He can be really quite funny sometimes.

ALAN. I suppose so. If you find that sort of thing amusing. He just seems like such a goddamn little pansy. (*Silence. A pause. He steps away.*) I'm sorry I said that.

I didn't mean to say that. That's such an awful thing to say about *anyone*. But you know what I mean, Michael—you have to admit he *is* effeminate.

MICHAEL. He is a bit.

ALAN. A bit! He's like a . . . a butterfly in heat! I mean there's no wonder he was trying to teach you all a dance. He *probably* wanted to dance *with* you! (*Crosses to* MICHAEL.) Oh, come on, man, you know me—you know how I feel—your private life is your own affair. (*Sits bed chair.*)

MICHAEL. (*Icy.*) No. I *don't* know that-about-you.

ALAN. I couldn't care less what people do—as long as they don't do it in public—or—or try to force their ways on the whole damned world.

MICHAEL. Alan, what was it you were crying about on the telephone?

ALAN. Oh, I feel like such a fool about that. I could shoot myself for letting myself act that way. I'm so embarrassed I could die.

MICHAEL. But Alan, if you were genuinely upset—that's nothing to be embarrassed about.

ALAN. All I can say is—please accept my apology for making such an ass of myself.

MICHAEL. You must have been upset or you wouldn't have said you were and that you wanted to see me—*had* to see me and had to talk to me.

ALAN. Can you forget it? Just pretend it never happened. I know *I* have. Okay?

MICHAEL. Is something wrong between you and Fran?

ALAN. Listen, I've really got to go. (*Rises and crosses Left of* MICHAEL.)

MICHAEL. (*Rises, counters Right to chair.*) Why are you in New York?

ALAN. I'm dreadfully late for dinner.

MICHAEL. *Whose* dinner? Where are you going?

ALAN. Is this the loo?

MICHAEL. Yes.

ALAN. Excuse me. (*He quickly goes into the bathroom.*)

(MICHAEL *remains silent, stares into space; sits on bed.
Downstairs*, EMORY *pops in from the kitchen to discover* DONALD *and* LARRY *in quiet, intimate conversation.*)

EMORY.   What's-going-on-in-here-oh-Mary-don't-ask!
(*He puts napkin holder on the table at Left.*)

(HANK *enters, carrying a bottle of red wine, from kitchen
and goes to bar for corkscrew. He looks toward*
LARRY *and* DONALD. DONALD *sees him.*)

DONALD. Hank, why don't you come and join us?
HANK. That's an interesting suggestion. Whose idea is
that?
DONALD. Mine.
LARRY. (*To* HANK.) He means in a conversation.

(BERNARD *enters from the kitchen, carrying two wine
glasses, without sport coat on.*)

EMORY. (*To* BERNARD.) Where're the rest of the wine
glasses? (*Catching* BERNARD *at Center.*)
BERNARD. Ahz workin' as fas' as ah can! (*A la Butterfly McQueen.*)

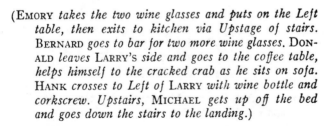

EMORY. They have to be told everything. Can't let 'em
out of your sight.

(EMORY *takes the two wine glasses and puts on the Left
table, then exits to kitchen via Upstage of stairs.*
BERNARD *goes to bar for two more wine glasses.* DONALD *leaves* LARRY'S *side and goes to the coffee table,
helps himself to the cracked crab as he sits on sofa.*
HANK *crosses to Left of* LARRY *with wine bottle and
corkscrew. Upstairs,* MICHAEL *gets up off the bed
and goes down the stairs to the landing.*)

HANK. I thought maybe you were abiding by the agreement.

LARRY. We have no agreement.

HANK. We *did*.

LARRY. *You* did. I never agreed to anything!

(LARRY *rises and goes above sofa and sits Down Right chair.* HANK *takes wine to Left table, finishes uncorking and sits in Down Left chair.* DONALD *looks up to see* MICHAEL *on landing and raises a crab claw toward him.*)

DONALD. To your health.

MICHAEL. Up yours.

DONALD. Up my health?

BERNARD. Where's the gent?

MICHAEL. (*Coming down stairs.*) In the gents' room. If you can all hang on for five more minutes, he's about to leave.

(*The DOOR buzzes.* MICHAEL *crosses to it.*)

LARRY. Well, at last!

(MICHAEL *opens the door to reveal a muscle-bound young* MAN, *wearing boots, tight levis, a calico neckerchief, and a cowboy hat. Around his wrist there is a large card tied with a string.*)

COWBOY. (*Singing fast.*)
      "Happy birthday to you,
      Happy birthday to you,
      Happy birthday, dear Harold.
      Happy birthday to you."

(*And with that, he gives* MICHAEL *a big kiss on the lips.* EMORY *enters from kitchen.*)

MICHAEL. Who the hell are you?

EMORY. She's Harold's present from me and she's *early!*

(*Quick to* COWBOY.) And that's not even Harold, you *idiot!*

(*He pushes* COWBOY *Down Left Center as* MICHAEL *closes the door and crosses to Right end of sofa.*)

COWBOY. You said whoever answered the door.

EMORY. But *not until midnight!* (*Quickly to* GROUP.) He's supposed to be a *midnight cowboy!*

DONALD. He *is* a midnight cowboy.

MICHAEL. He looks right out of a William Inge play to me.

EMORY. (*To* COWBOY.) . . . Not until midnight and you're supposed to sing to the right person, for Chrissake! I *told* you Harold has very, very, tight, tight, black curly hair. (*Referring to* MICHAEL.) This number's practically bald!

MICHAEL. Thank you and fuck you.

BERNARD. It's a good thing *I* didn't open the door.

EMORY. Not that tight and not that black.

COWBOY. I forgot. Besides, I wanted to get to the bars by midnight.

MICHAEL. He's a class act all the way around.

EMORY. What do you mean—get to the bars! Sweetie, I paid you for the whole night, remember?

COWBOY. I hurt my back doing my exercises and I wanted to get to bed early tonight.

BERNARD. Are you ready for this one?

LARRY. (*To* COWBOY.) That's too bad, what happened?

COWBOY. I lost my grip doing my chin-ups and I fell on my heels and twisted my back.

EMORY. You shouldn't *wear* heels when you do chin-ups.

COWBOY. (*Oblivious.*) I shouldn't do chin-ups—I got a weak grip to begin with.

EMORY. A weak grip. In my day it used to be called a limp wrist.

BERNARD. Who can remember that far back?

MICHAEL. (*To* LARRY.) Who was it that always used to

say, "You show me Oscar Wilde in a cowboy suit, and I'll
show you a gay caballero."

DONALD. I don't know. Who *was* it who always used
to say that?

MICHAEL. I don't know. Somebody. (*Crosses above
sofa.*)

LARRY. (*To* COWBOY.) What does your card say?

COWBOY. (*Holds up his wrist crossing to* LARRY.) Here.
You read it.

LARRY. (*Rises. Reading card.*) "Dear Harold, bang,
bang, you're alive. But roll-over and play dead. Happy
Birthday, Emory."

(ALAN *enters from bath and comes down the stairs.*)

BERNARD. Ah, sheer poetry, Emmy.

LARRY. And in your usual good taste. (*Sits chair.*)

MICHAEL. Yes, so conservative of you to resist a sign in
Times Square.

EMORY. (*Glancing toward stairs.*) Cheese it! Here
comes the socialite nun. (*Goes to high stool and sits.*)

MICHAEL. Goddammit, Emory! (*Crosses to* EMORY.)

ALAN. (*On bottom step.*) Well, I'm off. . . . Thanks,
Michael, for the drink.

MICHAEL. You're entirely welcome, Alan. See you tomorrow?

ALAN. . . . No. No, I think I'm going to be awfully
busy. I may even go back to Washington.

EMORY. Got a heavy date in La Fayette Square?

ALAN. What?

HANK. Emory.

EMORY. Forget it.

ALAN. (*Sees* COWBOY *and crosses Down Left Center.*)
Are you . . . Harold?

EMORY. No, he's not Harold. He's *for* Harold.

(*Silence.* ALAN *lets it pass. Turns to* HANK *and crosses
to him.* MICHAEL *gets on first step, glaring at*
EMORY.)

ALAN. Goodbye, Hank. It was nice to meet you.
HANK. (*Rises.*) Same here.

(*They shake hands.*)

ALAN. If you're ever in Washington—I'd like you to
meet my wife.
HANK. Good.

(ALAN *starts for the door, crossing Up Center.*)

LARRY. That'd be fun, wouldn't it, Hank?
EMORY. Yeah, they'd love to meet him—*her.* I have
such a problem with pronouns.
ALAN. (*Quick, to* EMORY.) How many esses are there in
the word pronoun?
EMORY. How'd you like to kiss my ass—that's got two
or more *essessss* in it!
ALAN. How'd you like to blow me!
EMORY. What's the matter with your *wife,* she got lock-
jaw?
ALAN. (*Lashes out.*) Faggot, Fairy, pansy . . .
(*Lunges at* EMORY, *grabs him, pulls him off stool to floor
and attacks him fiercely.*) queer, cocksucker! I'll kill you,
you goddamn little mincing, swish! You goddamn freak!
FREAK! FREAK!

(*Pandemonium!* EVERYONE *overlaps words.* ALAN *has
quickly beaten* EMORY *to the floor before anyone has
recovered from the surprise, and reacted to move.*)

EMORY. Oh, my God, somebody help me! Bernard! He's
killing me!

(BERNARD *and* HANK *rush forward.* EMORY *is screaming.*)

HANK. Alan! ALAN! *ALAN!*

(*Pulls* ALAN *off* EMORY *via above sofa and gets* ALAN
Down Right on floor.)

EMORY. Get him off me! Get him off me! Oh, my God,
he's broken my nose! I'm BLEEDING TO DEATH!

(BERNARD *quickly bends over* EMORY, *puts his arm
around him and lifts him to Down Left where* EMORY
falls to the floor.)

BERNARD. Somebody get some ice! And a cloth!

(LARRY *runs to the bar, grabs the bar towel and the ice
bucket, rushes to put it on the floor beside* BERNARD
and EMORY. BERNARD *quickly wraps some ice in the
towel, holds it to* EMORY's *mouth.*)

EMORY. Oh, my face!
BERNARD. He busted your lip, that's all. It'll be all
right.

(HANK *has gotten* ALAN *down on the floor on the opposite
side of the room.* ALAN *relinquishes the struggle.*
MICHAEL *is still standing on the first step, immobile.*)

DONALD. (*Rises. To* COWBOY.) Would you mind wait-
ing over there with the gifts? (*The front door BUZZER
sounds.* DONALD *has crossed to high stool, which is the
gift-wrapped packages area, and indicates for the* COWBOY
to sit there and DONALD *continues to move to answer the
door, opens it to reveal* HAROLD.) Well, Harold! Happy
Birthday. (HAROLD *is entering the room getting near* COW-
BOY *at Center but too busy taking in the room to see him.*)
You're just in time for the floor show which, as you see, is
on the floor. (*To* COWBOY.) Hey, you, *this* is Harold!

(HAROLD *looks at* COWBOY—COWBOY *rises and sings.*)

COWBOY.
> "Happy birthday to you,
> Happy birthday to you,
> Happy birthday, dear Harold.
> Happy birthday to you."
> (*And he gives* HAROLD *a big kiss.*)

(DONALD *has gone to the phonograph and turns on MUSIC as* COWBOY *finishes singing.* HAROLD *breaks away from* COWBOY, *reads the card, begins to laugh, continues to laugh.* MICHAEL, *as* COWBOY *finishes singing, walks to the bar, pours a glass of gin, raises it to his lips as the LIGHTS dim out to a SPOT pointing up* MICHAEL'S *first drink.* DONALD *watches silently as* HAROLD *continues to laugh and SPOT dims to black.*)

CURTAIN

ACT TWO

A moment later. HAROLD *is still laughing.* MICHAEL, *still at the bar, lowers his glass, turns to* DONALD, *indicates for him to cut PHONOGRAPH which he does.*

MICHAEL. What's so fucking funny?

HAROLD. (*Unintimidated.*) Life. Life is a god-damn laff-riot. You remember life.

MICHAEL. *You're stoned.*

LARRY. Happy Birthday, Harold.

MICHAEL. (*To* HAROLD.) You're stoned and you're late! You were supposed to arrive at this location at approximately eight-thirty dash nine o'clock!

HAROLD. What I *am,* Michael, is a thirty-two year old, ugly, pock-marked Jew Fairy—and if it takes me a while to pull myself together and if I smoke a little grass before I can get up the nerve to show my face to the world, it's nobody's god-damn business but my own. (*Instant switch to chatty tone.*) And how are *you* this evening?

(HANK *lifts* ALAN *to the sofa and both sit.* COWBOY *sits on fourth step of stairs.* MICHAEL *turns away from* HAROLD, *pours himself another drink.* DONALD *watches.*)

EMORY. Happy Birthday, Hallie. (*Now wearing a bloody sweater.*)

HAROLD. What happened to *you?*

EMORY. (*Groans.*) Don't ask!

HAROLD. Your lips are turning blue—you look like you been rimming a snowman.

(LARRY *rises and returns ice bucket to bar and sits Down Right chair.*)

48

EMORY. (*Indicating* ALAN.) That piss-elegant **kooze** hit me!

(BERNARD *helps* EMORY *up from the floor to sit him in Down Left chair.* HAROLD *looks toward the sofa.* ALAN *has slumped forward with hands over his ears.*)

MICHAEL. Careful, Emory, that kind of talk just makes him s'nervous.

HAROLD. (*crosses to Left end sofa to* ALAN.) Who is she? Who was she? Who does she hope to be?

EMORY. Who knows, who cares!

HANK. His name is Alan McCarthy.

MICHAEL. Do forgive me for not formally introducing you.

HAROLD. (*Sarcastically to* MICHAEL.) Not the famous college *chum.*

MICHAEL. (*Takes an ice cube from ice bucket, throws it up and catches it.*) Do a figure eight on that. (*Puts ice in his glass.*)

HAROLD. Well, well, well. I finally get to meet dear ole Alan after all these years. And in black-tie too. Is this my surprise from you, Michael?

LARRY. I think Alan is the one who got the surprise.

DONALD. And, if you'll notice, he's absolutely speechless. (*Crosses to above sofa.*)

EMORY. I *hope* she's in *shock!* She's a beast!

COWBOY. (*Indicating* ALAN.) Is it his birthday too?

EMORY. (*Indicates* COWBOY *to* HAROLD. *Rises and brings* COWBOY *to Down Left Center.*) *That's* your surprise.

LARRY. Speaking of beasts.

(BERNARD *sits in Down Right chair.*)

EMORY. From me to you, darlin'. How do you like it?
HAROLD. (*Crosses to* COWBOY.) Oh, I suppose he **has**

an interesting face and body--but it turns me right off because he can't talk intelligently about art.

EMORY. Yeah, ain't it a shame?

(COWBOY *goes to ottoman and sits.*)

HAROLD. I could never *love* anyone like that. (*Going to* EMORY.)

EMORY. Never. *Who could?*

HAROLD. *I* could and *you* could, that's who could! Oh, Mary, she's *gorgeous!*

EMORY. She may be dumb, but she's all yours!

HAROLD. In affairs of the heart there are no rules! Where'd you ever find him? (*Crossing to* COWBOY.)

EMORY. Rae knew where.

MICHAEL. (*To* DONALD.) Rae is Rae Clark. That's R.A.*E*. She's Emory's dike friend who sings at a place in the Village. She wears pin-striped suits and bills herself, "Miss Rae Clark—Songs Tailored To Your Taste."

(COWBOY *picks up crab tray and investigates.*)

EMORY. Rae's a fabulous chanteuse. I adore the way she does "Down In The Depths On The Ninetieth Floor."

MICHAEL. The faggot national anthem. (*Exits to the kitchen with soda glass.*)

HAROLD. (*To* EMORY.) All I can say is thank God for Miss Rae Clark. (*Goes to* EMORY.) I think my present is a super surprise! I'm so thrilled to get it I'd kiss you but I don't want to get blood all over me.

EMORY. Ohhh, look at my sweater!

(BERNARD *rises and goes to* EMORY.)

HAROLD. Wait'll you see your face.

BERNARD. Come on, Emory, let's clean you up. Happy Birthday, Harold. (*Follows* EMORY *upstairs.*)

HAROLD. (*Smiles.*) Thanks, love. (*Goes to Left table.*)

(MICHAEL *enters from kitchen.*)

EMORY. My sweater is ruined!

MICHAEL. Take one of mine in the bedroom.

DONALD. The one on the floor is vicuna.

(COWBOY *rises and exits to kitchen with cracked crab.*)

BERNARD. (*To* EMORY.) You'll feel better after I bathe your face. (BERNARD *and* EMORY *exit to bath.*)

HAROLD. Just another birthday party with the folks.

MICHAEL. (*He has a wine bottle and a green crystal white wine glass. Going to* HAROLD.) Here's a cold bottle of Puilly-Fuisse I bought especially for you, kiddo. (*Pours a glass.*)

HAROLD. Pussycat, all is forgiven. You can stay. (*Takes glass.*) No. You can stay, but not all is forgiven. Cheers. (*Sits Down Left chair.*)

MICHAEL. I didn't want it this way, Hallie. (*Puts wine bottle on Left table.*)

(DONALD *crosses to Left of stairs.*)

HAROLD. (*Indicating* ALAN.) Who asked Mr. Right to celebrate my birthday?

DONALD. There are no accidents.

HAROLD. (*Referring to* DONALD.) And who asked *him?*

MICHAEL. *Guilty again.*

HAROLD. Always got to have your crutch, haven't you.

DONALD. I'm *not* leaving.

HAROLD. Nobody ever thinks completely of somebody else. They always please themselves, they always cheat, if only a little bit.

LARRY. (*Referring to* ALAN.) Why is he sitting there with his hands over his ears?

DONALD. I think he has an ick.

(DONALD *looks at* MICHAEL—MICHAEL *returns it, steely and goes above sofa.*)

HANK. (*To* ALAN.) Can I get you a drink?

LARRY. How can he hear you, dummy, with his hands over his ears?

HAROLD. He can hear every word. In fact, he wouldn't miss a word if it killed him. (ALAN *removes his hands from his ears.*) What'd I tell you?

ALAN. (*Rises.*) I . . . I . . . feel sick. I think . . . I'm going to . . . throw up.

HANK. This way. (*Rises and takes* ALAN *to landing of stairs.*)

HAROLD. Say that again and I won't have to take my appetite depressant.

(BERNARD *and* EMORY *come out of the bath.*)

BERNARD. There. Feel better?

EMORY. Oh, Mary, what would I do without you? (EMORY *looks at himself in the mirror.*) I am not ready for my close-up, Mr. De Mille. Nor will I be for the next two weeks.

(BERNARD *picks up* MICHAEL'S *sweater.*)

ALAN. I'm going to throw up! Let me go! Let me go! (*He tears loose of* HANK, *bolts up the remainder of the stairs to bath.* HANK *follows.*)

(EMORY *lets out a scream as* ALAN *rushes toward him.*)

EMORY. Oh, my God, he's after me again! (EMORY *jumps over bed.*)

HANK. He's sick.

BERNARD. Yeah, sick in the head. Here, Emory, put this on. (*Going to* EMORY *with vicuna sweater.*)

EMORY. (*Sits on bench.*) Oh, Mary, take me home. My nerves can't stand any more of this tonight. (EMORY *takes the sweater from* BERNARD, *starts to put it on.*)

(*Downstairs, at same time,* HAROLD *flamboyantly takes*

out a cigarette, takes a match from a striker and crosses to Center of sofa.)

HAROLD. TURNING ON! (*With that, he strikes the match and lights up. Through a strained throat.*) Anybody care to join me? (*He waves the cigarette in a slow pass.*)

(COWBOY *enters from kitchen.*)

MICHAEL. Many thanks, no.
DONALD. No, thank you.
HAROLD. (*To* COWBOY.) How about you, Tex?
COWBOY. Yeah. (*Sits ottoman with pot cigarette.*)
MICHAEL. I find the sound of the ritual alone, utterly humiliating. (*He turns away.*)

(EMORY *and* BERNARD *come downstairs.*)

LARRY. I hate the smell poppers leave on your fingers.
HAROLD. Why don't you get up and wash your hands?

(EMORY *is on bottom step and* BERNARD *is on landing.*)

EMORY. Michael, I left the casserole in the oven. You can take it out any time.
MICHAEL. You're not going. (*Picks up gin.*)
EMORY. I couldn't eat now anyway.
HAROLD. Well, *I'm* absolutely ravenous. I'm going to eat until I have a fat attack.
MICHAEL. (*To* EMORY.) I said, you're *not going.* (*Crosses to Right end of sofa with gin.*)
HAROLD. (*To* MICHAEL.) Having a cocktail this evening, are we? In my honor?
EMORY. It's your favorite dinner, Hallie. I made it myself.
BERNARD. *Who* fixed the casserole?
EMORY. Well; *I* made the sauce!

BERNARD. Well, *I* made the salad!

LARRY. Girls, please.

MICHAEL. Please *what!* (*Returns gin to bar.*)

HAROLD. Beware the hostile fag. When he's sober he's dangerous, when he drinks, he's lethal.

MICHAEL. (*Referring to* HAROLD.) Attention must *not* be paid. (*Paces to above sofa.*)

HAROLD. I'm starved, Em, I'm ready for some of your Alice B. Toklas's opium baked Lasagna.

EMORY. Are you really? Oh, that makes me so pleased maybe I'll just serve it before I leave. (EMORY *exits kitchen.*)

MICHAEL. *You're not leaving.* (*Crosses to desk.*)

BERNARD. I'll help. (*Starts for kitchen.*)

LARRY. (*Rises and exits kitchen.*) I better help too. We don't need a nose-bleed in the Lasagna.

BERNARD. When the sauce is on it you wouldn't be able to tell the difference anyway. (*Exits kitchen.*)

MICHAEL. (*Proclamation.*) Nobody's going anywhere! (*Goes to high stool and puts in front of front door.*)

HAROLD. You are going to have schmertz tomorrow you wouldn't believe.

MICHAEL. (*Crosses to bar for drink.*) May I kiss the hem of your schemata, Doctor Freud?

COWBOY. What are you two talking about? I don't understand.

(HANK *enters from bath and comes to landing.*)

DONALD. (*Crossing above sofa.*) He's working through his Oedipus Complex, sugar. With a machete.

COWBOY. Huh?

HANK. Michael, is there any air spray? (*On landing.*)

HAROLD. Hair spray! You're supposed to be holding his head, not doing his hair.

HANK. *Air* spray, not *hair* spray.

(DONALD *goes to bar, pours drink out of martini pitcher.*)

MICHAEL. (*Crosses below coffee table to steps with his drink.*) There's a can of floral spray right on top of the john.

HANK. Thanks. (HANK *goes back upstairs leaving his suit coat on bedroom bench as he exits into the bath.*)

HAROLD. (*To* MICHAEL.) Aren't you going to say, "If it was a snake, it would have bitten you."

MICHAEL. (*Indicating* COWBOY.) That is something only your friend would say.

HAROLD. (*To* MICHAEL.) I am turning-on and you are just turning. (MICHAEL *and* HAROLD *look at each other for a beat*—MICHAEL *decides to break to Left of stairs. To* DONALD.) I keep my grass in the medicine cabinet. In a Band-Aid box. Somebody told me it's the safest place. If the cops arrive you can always lock yourself in the bathroom and flush it down the john. (HAROLD *has removed his eye glasses.*)

DONALD. (*Takes* HAROLD'S *glasses and puts them on Upstage end of bar.*) Very cagey.

HAROLD. It makes more sense than where I *was* keeping it—in an oregano jar in the spice rack. I kept forgetting and accidentally turning my hateful mother on with the salad. (*A beat.*) But I think she liked it. No matter what meal she comes over for—even if it's breakfast—she says, "Let's have a salad!"

(HAROLD *looks to* MICHAEL, *and* MICHAEL *goes to Down Left chair and sits as* COWBOY *rises and crosses to* MICHAEL.)

COWBOY. (*To* MICHAEL.) Why do you say, I would say, "If it was a snake it would have bitten you"? I think that's what I *would* have said.

MICHAEL. Of course you would have, baby. That's the kind of remark your pint-size brain thinks of. You are definitely the type who still moves his lips when he reads and who sits in a steam room and says things like, "Hot enough for you?"

COWBOY. I never use the steam room when I go to the gym. It's bad after a work-out. It flattens you down.

MICHAEL. Just after you've broken your back to blow yourself up like a poisoned dog.

COWBOY. Yeah. (*Crosses to ottoman and sits.*)

(DONALD *goes to Down Right chair and sits.*)

MICHAEL. You're right, Harold. Not only can he not talk intelligently about art, he can't even follow from one sentence to the next.

HAROLD. *But he's beautiful.* He has *unnatural*, natural beauty. Not that that means anything.

MICHAEL. It doesn't mean *everything*.

HAROLD. Keep telling yourself that as your hair drops out in handfuls. (*Rises and crosses to* MICHAEL.) Not that it's not *natural* for one's hair to recede as one reaches seniority. Not that those wonderful lines that have begun creasing our countenances don't make all the difference in the world because they add so much *character*.

MICHAEL. Faggots are worse than women about their age. They think their lives are over at thirty. Physical beauty is not that god-damned important!

HAROLD. Of course not. How could it be?—it's only in the eye of the beholder.

MICHAEL. And it's only skin deep—don't forget that one.

HAROLD. Oh, no, I haven't forgotten that one at all. It's only skin deep and it's *transitory* too. It's *terribly* transitory. (*Crosses to* COWBOY.) I mean, how long does it last?—thirty or forty or fifty years at the most—depending on how well you take care of yourself. And not counting, of course, that you might die before it runs out anyway. Yes, it's too bad about this poor boy's face. It's tragic. He's absolutely cursed! (COWBOY *looks to* HAROLD.) How can *his* beauty ever compare with *my* soul? And although I have never seen my soul, I understand from my mother's rabbi that it's a knock-out. (*Crosses to*

Left table.) I, however, cannot seem to locate it for a gander. And if I could, I'd sell it in a flash for some skin-deep, transitory, meaningless beauty! (*Picks up wine bottle and glass.*)

MICHAEL. (*Makes sign of the cross with his drink in hand.*) Forgive him, Father, for he know not what he do. (*He rises and crosses to pillar at Center.*)

(*Upstairs,* ALAN *walks weakly into bedroom and lies down on bed.*)

HAROLD. Michael, you kill me. You don't know what side of the fence you're on. (LARRY *enters from kitchen via stair passage with silverware to Left table.*) If somebody says something pro-religion, you're against them. (LARRY *gives two clicks of silverware which makes* HAROLD *move out of way to stairs as* LARRY *puts silver on table.*) If somebody denies God, you're against *them.* One might say that you have some problem in that area. You can't live with it and you can't live without it.

(EMORY *enters from kitchen via Up Center carrying the hot casserole with pot holders, crossing to* MICHAEL, *who has arm up leaning on pillar blocking* EMORY's *passage.*)

EMORY. Hot stuff! Comin' through!

(LARRY *crosses to sofa and sits.*)

MICHAEL. (*To* EMORY.) One could murder you with very little effort.

(*Lets arm down so* EMORY *can pass and put casserole on Left table.*)

HAROLD. (*To* MICHAEL.) You hang onto that great insurance policy called The Church.

Pascal's wager

MICHAEL. (*Crossing above sofa.*) That's right. I believe in God and if it turns out that there really isn't one, okay. Nothing lost. But if it turns out that there *is*—I'm covered.

(BERNARD *enters carrying a salad bowl from kitchen Up Center and puts on Left table.*)

EMORY. (*To* MICHAEL.) Harriet Hypocrite, that's who you are.

MICHAEL. (*Going to bar.*) Right. I'm one of those truly rotten Catholics who gets drunk, sins all night and goes to Mass the next morning.

(EMORY *and* BERNARD *move Left table out from wall.*)

EMORY. Gilda Guilt. It depends on what you think sin is.

MICHAEL. Would you just shut-up your god-damn minty mouth and get back in the god-damn kitchen!   ^

EMORY. Say anything you want—*just don't hit me!* (*He exits into kitchen with pot holders via Up Center.*)

MICHAEL. Actually, I suppose Emory has a point—I only go to confession before I get on a plane.

BERNARD. Do you think God's power only exists at thirty thousand feet? (*Lights candles.*)

(HANK *enters from bath, retrieves his coat.*)

MICHAEL. It must. On the ground I *am* God. In the air, I'm just one more scared son-of-a-bitch.

BERNARD. I'm scared on the ground.

(HANK *hits bedroom LIGHT SWITCH and comes down steps to sofa.*)

COWBOY. Me too. That is, when I'm not high on pot or up on acid.

(BERNARD *pours wine.*)

LARRY. (*To* HANK.) Well, is it bigger than a bread-stick?

HANK. (*Ignores last remark; to* MICHAEL.) He's lying down for a minute. (*Lowers sleeves and puts on coat.*)

HAROLD. How does the bathroom smell?

HANK. Better.

MICHAEL. Before it smelled like somebody puked. Now it smells like somebody puked in a gardenia patch.

(EMORY *enters from kitchen via Up Center with rolls going to Left table.*)

LARRY. And how does the big hero feel?

HANK. Lay off, will you.

EMORY. *Dinner is served!*

HAROLD. (*He comes to the buffet table, puts down wine and glass and picks up plate, fork and napkin.*) Emory, it looks absolutely fabulous.

EMORY. I'd make somebody a good wife. (DONALD *rises and notes* MICHAEL *pouring another gin as he puts ice in his own drink.* EMORY *serves pasta,* BERNARD *serves the salad.* HANK, *with coat on, goes to Left table, followed by* LARRY.) I could cook and do an apartment and enter-tain . . . (*He grabs a long-stem rose from an arrange-ment on the table, clenches it between his teeth, snaps his fingers and strikes a pose.*) Kiss me quick, I'm Carmen! (HAROLD *just looks at him blankly and goes to Down Right chair and sits.* EMORY *takes the flower out of his mouth.*) One really needs castanets for that sort of thing.

(DONALD *crosses to* COWBOY *indicating for him to get in food line at Left table.*)

MICHAEL. And a getaway car.

(HANK *comes up to* EMORY.)

EMORY. What would you like, big boy?

LARRY. Alan McCarthy, and don't hold the mayo.

EMORY. I can't keep up with you two— (*Indicating* HANK, *then* LARRY.) I thought you were mad at him— now he's bitchin' you. What gives?

(HANK *takes his food and wine to sofa and sits.*)

LARRY. Never mind.

COWBOY. (*He comes over to the table.*) What is it?

LARRY. Lasagna.

COWBOY. (*To* DONALD.) It looks like spaghetti and meatballs sorta flattened out.

DONALD. It's been in the steam room.

COWBOY. It has?

(LARRY *crosses to ottoman and sits with his food.*)

MICHAEL. (*Contemptuously.*) It looks like spaghetti and meatballs sorta flattened out. Ah, yes, Harold—truly enviable.

(COWBOY *goes to stairs and sits on third step with his food.*)

HAROLD. As opposed to you who knows so much about haute cuisine. Raconteur, gourmet, troll.

COWBOY. It's good.

HAROLD. (*Quick.*) You like it, eat it.

MICHAEL. Stuff your mouth so that you can't say anything.

(DONALD *takes a plate.*)

HAROLD. Turning.

(MICHAEL *crosses via above sofa to* DONALD *at stairs.*)

BERNARD. (*To* DONALD.) Wine?

DONALD. No thanks. (*Crosses to* MICHAEL *at stairs with his drink and food.*)

(BERNARD *hands* EMORY *a plate, which* EMORY *puts food on.*)

MICHAEL. Aw, go on, kiddo, force yourself. Have a little vin ordinaire to wash down all that depressed pasta.

(DONALD *passes by and sits on high stool at door as* MICHAEL *goes to Left table.*)

HAROLD. Somelier, connoisseur, pig.

(EMORY *hands* BERNARD *a plate he has served with food.*)

BERNARD. (*To* EMORY.) Aren't you going to have any?

EMORY. No. My lip hurts too much to eat.

(BERNARD *sits Down Left chair with his plate.*)

MICHAEL. (*Crosses to table, picks up knife.*) I hear if you puts a knife under de bed it cuts de pain.

HAROLD. (*To* MICHAEL.) I hear if you put a knife under your chin it cuts your throat.

EMORY. Anybody going to take a plate up to Alan?

MICHAEL. The punching bag has now dissolved into Flo Nightingale.

LARRY. Hank?

HANK. I don't think he'd have any appetite.

(MICHAEL *raps the knife on a wine bottle.*)

MICHAEL. Ladies and gentlemen. . . . Correction: Ladies and ladies, I would like to announce that you have just eaten Sebastian Veneble. (*Puts knife on table.*)

COWBOY. Just eaten *what?*

MICHAEL. (*Goes to* COWBOY.) Not *what*, stupid, *who*. A character in a play. A fairy who was eaten alive. I mean the chop-chop variety.

COWBOY. Jesus. (*Puts plate down on steps.*)

(MICHAEL *crosses to sofa.*)

HANK. Did Edward Albee write that play?

MICHAEL. No. Tennessee Williams.

HANK. Oh, yeah.

MICHAEL. Albee wrote "Who's Afraid of Virginia Woolf?"

LARRY. Dummy.

HANK. I know that. I just thought maybe he wrote that other one too.

LARRY. Well, you made a mistake.

HANK. So I made a mistake.

LARRY. That's right, you made a mistake.

HANK. What's the difference? You can't add.

(BERNARD *laughs.*)

COWBOY. Edward who?

MICHAEL. (*To* EMORY.) How much did you pay for him?

EMORY. He was a steal.

MICHAEL. He's a ham sandwich—fifty cents any time of the day or night. (*Crosses to bar via below coffee table.*)

(DONALD *rises, crosses to Left table with plate.*)

HAROLD. King of the Pig People.

(MICHAEL *gives him a look.*)

EMORY. (*To* DONALD.) Would you like some more?

DONALD. No, thank you, Emory. It was very good.

EMORY. Did you like it?

COWBOY. I'm not a steal. I cost twenty dollars.

(DONALD *returns to stool.* BERNARD *returns his plate to*
     EMORY.)

EMORY. More?
BERNARD. (*Nods negatively.*) It was delicious—even if
I did make it myself.
EMORY. Isn't anybody having seconds?

(EMORY *bends over to whisper "cake" to* BERNARD. BER-
     NARD *goes to* COWBOY *and beckons him to follow him*
     out to the kitchen. COWBOY *exits with his plate to*
     kitchen.)

HAROLD. I'm having seconds and thirds and maybe even
fifths. (*He rises and crosses to* EMORY.) I'm absolutely
desperate to keep the weight up.
MICHAEL. (*Parodying* HAROLD.) You're *absolutely* paranoid about *absolutely* everything.
HAROLD. Oh, yeah, well, why don't you *not* tell me
about it? (*Returns to his chair.*)
MICHAEL. (*Crosses above sofa.*) You starve yourself all
day, living on coffee and cottage cheese so that you can
gorge yourself at one meal. Then you feel guilty and moan
and groan about how fat you are and how ugly you are
when the truth is you're no fatter or thinner than you ever
are.
EMORY. Polly Paranoia. (EMORY *moves to the coffee*
table to take HANK'S *empty plate.*)
HANK. Just great, Emory. Thanks.
EMORY. Connie Casserole, no-trouble-at-all-oh-Mary,
D.A.

(*Takes* HANK'S *plate to Left table, and* LARRY *follows*
     EMORY *with his plate.*)

MICHAEL. (*Crossing to* HAROLD.) . . . And this patho-
logical lateness. It's downright *crazy.*
HAROLD. Turning.

(EMORY *exits into kitchen via stairs with dirty plates.*)

MICHAEL. Standing before a bathroom mirror for hours and hours before you can walk out on the street. And looking no different af:er Christ knows how many applications of Christ knows how many ointments and salves and creams and masks.

(LARRY *nods to* HANK *to help put table back to wall, which* HANK *is slow to respond to.*)

HAROLD. I've got bad skin, what can I tell you?

MICHAEL. Who wouldn't after they deliberately take a pair of tweezers and *deliberately* mutilate their pores—no wonder you've got holes in your face after the hack-job you've done on yourself year in and year out!

(HANK *rises with wine glass and goes to Left table.*)

HAROLD. (*Coolly but aefinitely.*) You hateful sow.

(LARRY *and* HANK *move table to wall.* LARRY *sits down Left chair,* HANK *sits on steps.*)

MICHAEL. Yes, you've got scars on your face—but they're not that bad and if you'd leave yourself alone you wouldn't have any more than you've already awarded yourself.

HAROLD. You'd really like me to compliment you now for being so honest, wouldn't you? For being my best friend who will tell me what even my best friends won't tell me. Slut!

MICHAEL. And the pills! (*Announcement to* GROUP.) Harold has been gathering, saving and storing up barbiturates for the last year like a god-damn squirrel. Hundreds of nembutals, hundreds of seconals. All in preparation for and anticipation of the long winter of his death. (*Crossing via above coffee table to bar to pour another gin.*) But I tell you right now, Harold. When the time comes, you'll never have the guts. It's not always like it happens in plays, not all faggots bump themselves off at the end of the story.

HAROLD. (*Rises, taking plate to Left table.*) What you say may be true. Time will undoubtedly tell. But, in the meantime, you've left out one detail—the cosmetics and astringents are *paid* for, the bathroom is *paid* for, the tweezers are *paid* for, and the pills *are paid for!* (*Throws napkin on floor.*)

(EMORY *darts to the LIGHT SWITCH, plunges the room into DARKNESS, except for the light from the tapers on the buffet table, and begins to sing, "Happy Birthday." Immediately, the* COWBOY *enters carrying a cake ablaze with candles and goes to* HAROLD. BERNARD *follows* COWBOY *with his sport coat on.* EVERYONE *has now joined in: "Happy Birthday, dear Harold, Happy Birthday to you." This is followed by a round of applause as* HAROLD *sits on sofa.*)

EMORY. Blow out your candles, Mary, and make a wish!

MICHAEL. Blow out your candles, *Laura.*

(*The* COWBOY *has brought cake over in front of* HAROLD *He blows out the candles. More applause.*)

EMORY. Awwww, she's thirty-two years young!

(*The LIGHTS are restored.*)

HAROLD. Oh, my God!

(*The* COWBOY *takes the cake to the Left table.*)

HANK. (*Hands his sweater gift to* HAROLD *and goes above Center of sofa.*) Now you have to open your gifts.

(LARRY *has come over to the stairs during the singing and now is gathering all the gifts and takes them to* HAROLD.)

HAROLD. Oh, do I have to open them here?
LARRY. Open this one first.

(*Handing* HAROLD *the poster gift and taking* HANK's *gift back from* HAROLD *as* LARRY *sits next to* HAROLD *on sofa.*)

EMORY. Of course you've got to open them here. Where does she think she's gonna open them? (*He is crossing above sofa when he sees the card on the floor by the pillar and retrieves it.*)
HAROLD. (*Begins to rip the paper from poster gift.*) Where's the card?
EMORY. Here. (*Hands card to* HAROLD *as he sits on ottoman.*)
HAROLD. Oh. From Larry. (ALL *groan "aahhh" as* HAROLD *finishes tearing off the tissue paper. While* HAROLD *is tearing paper* MICHAEL *gets cigarettes from coffee table and lights up one at the bar, which* DONALD *takes note of.*) It's *heaven!* I just love it, Larry.
COWBOY. What is it? (*Crossing to steps.*)
HAROLD. It's the deed to Boardwalk.

(HAROLD *holds up a graphic design: a large-scale "Deed to Boardwalk," like those used in a Monopoly game.* LARRY *puts ripped-off tissue from gift under sofa.*)

EMORY. Oh, gay pop art!
DONALD. (*To* LARRY.) It's sensational. Did you do it? (*At Right end of sofa.*)
LARRY. Yes.
HAROLD. Oh, it's super, Larry. It goes up the minute I get home.

(HAROLD *gives* LARRY *a kiss on the cheek as he hands "Boardwalk" to* EMORY.)

COWBOY. (*To* HAROLD.) I don't get it—you cruise Atlantic City or something?

MICHAEL. Will somebody get him out of here! (*Sits in Down Right chair.*)

(HAROLD *has opened another gift, takes the card from inside. The gift is a sweater.* EMORY *leans "Boardwalk" at Left End sofa.*)

HAROLD. Oh, what a nifty sweater! Thank you, Hank.

HANK. (*At above Center sofa.*) You can take it back and pick out another one if you want to.

HAROLD. I think this one is just nifty.

(HAROLD *gives sweater to* LARRY *with a look "ugly" as* LARRY *gives him the pad box and* LARRY *puts sweater box on floor next to "Boardwalk."*)

BERNARD. Who wants cake? (*At Right end of sofa.*)

EMORY. Everybody? (*Rises and goes to cake on buffet table.*)

(COWBOY *sits on ottoman.*)

DONALD. None for me.

MICHAEL. I'd just like to sleep on mine, thank you.

HAROLD. (*He has opened another gift, suddenly laughs aloud.*) Oh, Bernard! How divine! Look, everybody! Bejewelled knee-pads! (*He holds up a pair of basketball knee-pads with sequin initials.*)

BERNARD. Monogrammed!

EMORY. (*Crossing to* HAROLD.) Bernard, you're a camp! Let me see.

(HAROLD *hands pads to* EMORY. HAROLD *gives* LARRY *pad box and* LARRY *gives him* MICHAEL'S *gift.*)

MICHAEL. Y'all heard of Gloria De Haven and Billy De Wolfe, well, dis here is Rosemary De Camp!

BERNARD. Who?

EMORY. I never miss a Rosemary De Camp picture.

HANK. I've never heard of her.

COWBOY. Me neither.

HANK. Not all of us spent their childhood in a movie house, Michael. Some of us played baseball.

DONALD. And mowed the lawn.

EMORY. Well, *I* know who Rosemary De Camp is.

MICHAEL. You would. It's a cinch you wouldn't recognize a baseball or a lawnmower.

HAROLD. (*He has opened his last gift. He is silent.*) Thank you, Michael.

MICHAEL. What? (*Turns to see the gift.*) Oh. (*Rises, goes to bar and puts out cigarette.*) You're welcome. (*Gets his drink.*)

LARRY. What is it, Harold?

HAROLD. It's a photograph of him in a silver frame. And there's an inscription engraved and the date.

BERNARD. What's it say?

HAROLD. Just . . . something personal. (*Gives* LARRY *the gift.*)

MICHAEL. (*Turns round from the bar.*) Well, Bernard, what do you say we have a little music to liven things up!

(LARRY *hands* HANK *the sweater box and* HANK *pulls out the desk chair and puts it on the seat and lingers Up Center.* LARRY *also hands* DONALD *"Boardwalk" which he puts on desk chair and then goes to Down Left chair and sits.*)

BERNARD. Okay. (*Goes to phonograph.*)

EMORY. Yeah, I feel like dancing.

MICHAEL. (*Crosses above sofa.*) How about something good and ethnic, Emory?—one of your specialties like a military toe-tap with sparklers.

EMORY. (*Puts pads in box on coffee table and picks up his drink.*) I don't do that at birthdays—only on the Fourth of July.

(BERNARD *puts on RECORD and crosses to bar.* EMORY *goes to* BERNARD, *picking up* HAROLD'S *napkin from floor and puts in waste can and then joins* BERNARD *and starts to dance slowly.* HAROLD *lights a pot cigarette.* ALAN, *in se. ond floor bedroom, rises from bed and comes downstairs to landing.* LARRY *has taken the remaining gifts to the desk chair. Gives* HANK *a look before turning to* MICHAEL.)

LARRY. Come on, Michael.
MICHAEL. I can only lead.
LARRY. I can follow.

(LARRY *and* MICHAEL *start to dance above sofa.* HANK *exits into kitchen.* EMORY *gets pot cigarette from* HAROLD *while still dancing and shares it with* BERNARD.)

HAROLD. (*Rises and goes to* COWBOY.) Come on, Tex, you're on. (COWBOY *gets to his feet, but he is a washout as a dancing partner. He just stands still.* HAROLD *even tries to let him lead, but no good and so gives up.*) Later. (HAROLD *takes out another cigarette and a match as he crosses Left and catches sight of someone over by the stairs landing, walks over to* ALAN *and strikes a match.*) Wanna dance? (*Lights his cigarette.*)

EMORY. (*Sees* ALAN, *pronounces the following name:* "*E-von.*") Uh- oh. Ivan the terrible is back.
MICHAEL. (*Turns to* ALAN.) Oh, hello, Alan. Feel better? This is where you came in, isn't it? (ALAN *starts to cross down steps breaking away and giving* LARRY *his drink to hold.*) Excuse me, Larry. . . ., (ALAN *has reached the third step as* MICHAEL *intercepts, blocking* ALAN *with his foot.*) As they say in the Deep South, don't rush off in the heat of the day.
HAROLD. Revolution complete.
MICHAEL. . . . You missed the cake—and you missed the opening of the gifts—but you're still in luck. You're

just in time for a party game. . . . Hey, everybody!
Game time!

(MICHAEL *indicates to* BERNARD *to turn phonograph off,
   which he does. LARRY *takes* MICHAEL'S *drink to bar
   and sits on high stool at door.*)

HAROLD. Why don't you just let him go, Michael?

(*He crosses to Down Right chair and sits indicating to*
   COWBOY *to come over to him.* COWBOY *goes to*
   HAROLD *and sits on a cushion by* HAROLD'S *chair on
   the floor, where he removes his hat, card and kerchief.*)

MICHAEL. (*Crossing to Left of* ALAN.) He can go if
he wants to—but not before we play a game.

(ALAN *starts to move,* MICHAEL *catches him gently by
   the sleeve and tugs* ALAN *to sit.* ALAN *sits on third
   step.*)

EMORY. What's it going to be—movie star gin? (*Sits
on sofa.*)
MICHAEL. That's too faggy for Alan to play—he
wouldn't be any good at it.
BERNARD. (*Crosses to pillar and leans.*) What about
Likes and Dislikes?

(HANK *enters from kitchen and crosses Up Right near*
   LARRY.)

MICHAEL. (*Crosses to Left end sofa.*) It's too much
trouble to find enough pencils, and besides, Emory always
puts down the same thing. He dislikes artificial fruit and
flowers and coffee grinders made into lamps—and he likes
Mabel Mercer, poodles, and "All about Eve"—the screenplay of which he will then recite *verbatim.*

EMORY. I put down other things sometimes.

MICHAEL. Like a tan out of season?

EMORY. I just always put down little "Chi-Chi" because I adore her so much.

MICHAEL. If one is of the masculine gender, a poodle is the *insignia* of one's deviation. (*Goes to desk for pad and pencil.*)

BERNARD. (*Crosses in to* EMORY.) You know why old ladies like poodles—because they go down on them.

EMORY. *They do not.* (*Gives* BERNARD *a swat as* BERNARD *returns to pillar.*)

LARRY. We could play B For Botticelli.

MICHAEL. (*Crosses to Right end sofa.*) We *could* play *Spin* The Botticelli, but we're not going to.

HAROLD. What would you like to play, Michael—The Truth Game?

MICHAEL. (*He chuckles to himself.*) Cute, Hallie.

HAROLD. Or do you want to play Murder? You all remember that one, don't you?

MICHAEL. (*To* HAROLD.) Very, very cute.

DONALD. (*Rises and crosses to stairs, leaning on landing.*) As I recall, they're quite similar. The rules are the same in both—you kill somebody.

MICHAEL. (*Crosses to steps.*) In affairs of the heart, there are no rules. Isn't that right, Harold?

HAROLD. That's what I always say.

MICHAEL. Well, that's the name of the game. The Affairs Of The Heart.

COWBOY. I've never heard of that one.

MICHAEL. (*To* COWBOY.) Of course you've never heard of it—I just made it up, baby doll. (*To* ALL.) Affairs Of The Heart is a combination of both the Truth Game and Murder—with a new twist.

HAROLD. I can hardly wait to find out what that is.

ALAN. Mickey, I'm leaving. (*He starts to move, ending up Down Center.*)

MICHAEL. (*Firmly, flatly.*) Stay where you are.

HAROLD. Michael, let him go.

MICHAEL. (*Crosses to* ALAN.) He really doesn't *want to*. If he did, he'd have left a long time ago—or he wouldn't have come here in the first place.

ALAN. (*Holding his forehead.*) . . . Mickey, I don't *feel* well!

MICHAEL. (*Low tone but distinctly articulate.*) My name is Michael. I am called Michael. You must never call anyone called Michael, Mickey. Those of us who are named Michael are very nervous about it. If you don't believe it—try it.

ALAN. I'm sorry. I can't think. (*Starts to go.*)

MICHAEL. (*Stops* ALAN *by stepping in his way.*) You can think. What you can't do—is leave. It's like watching an accident on the highway—you can't look at it and you can't look away.

ALAN. I . . . feel . . . weak . . .

MICHAEL. You are weak. Much weaker than I think you realize. (ALAN *crosses to Down Left chair and sits.*) Now! Who's going to play with Alan and me? Everyone?

HAROLD. I have no intention of playing.

DONALD. Nor do I.

MICHAEL. Well, not everyone is a participant in life. There are always those who stand on the sidelines and watch.

LARRY. What's the game?

MICHAEL. (*Goes to desk and brings phone to Left end sofa.*) Simply this: We all have to call on the telephone the *one person* we truly believed we have loved.

HANK. (*Crosses in to above sofa.*) I'm not playing.

LARRY. Oh, yes you are.

HANK. (*Turns to* LARRY.) You'd like for me to play, wouldn't you?

LARRY. You bet I would. I'd like to know who you'd call after all the fancy speeches I've heard lately. Who would you call? Would you call me?

MICHAEL. (*To* BERNARD.) Sounds like there's, how you say, trouble in paradise.

HAROLD. If there isn't, I think you'll be able to stir up some.

HANK. (*Crosses to* LARRY.) And who would *you* call? Don't think I think for one minute it would be me. Or that one call would do it. You'd have to make several, wouldn't you? About three long distance and God-only-knows how many locals. (*Crosses below coffee table to Left table.*)

COWBOY. I'm glad I don't have to pay the bill.

MICHAEL. Quiet!

HAROLD. (*To* COWBOY.) Oh, don't worry, Michael won't pay it either.

MICHAEL. Now, here's how it works.

LARRY. I thought you said there were no rules.

MICHAEL. (*Crosses to* LARRY.) That's right. In Affairs Of The Heart, there are no rules. This is the god-damn point system! (*Crosses to Center.* DONALD *goes to steps and sits fourth step.* HANK *takes* DONALD's *place at landing.*) If you make the call, you get one point. If the person you are calling answers, you get two more points—if somebody else answers, you get only one. If there's no answer at all, you're screwed.

DONALD. You're screwed if you make the call.

HAROLD. You're a *fool*—if you screw yourself.

MICHAEL. . . . When you get the person whom you are calling on the line—if you tell them who you are, you get two points. And then—if you tell them that you *love* them —you get a bonus of five more points!

HAROLD. Hateful.

MICHAEL. Therefore you can get as many as ten points and as few as one.

HAROLD. You can get as few as none—if you know how to work it.

MICHAEL. The one with the highest score wins.

ALAN. Hank. Let's get out of here.

EMORY. Well, now. Did you hear that!

MICHAEL. Just the two of you together. The pals . . . the guys . . . the buddie-buddies . . . the he-men.

EMORY. I think Larry might have something to say about that.

BERNARD. Emory.

MICHAEL. (*Re: last remark.*) The duenna speaks. So who's playing? Excluding Cowboy, who, as a gift, is neuter. And, of course, la voyeurs. Emory? (*A beat.*) Bernard?

BERNARD. I don't think I want to play.

MICHAEL. Why, Bernard! Where's your fun-loving spirit?

BERNARD. I don't think this game is fun. (*Goes to ottoman and sits.*)

HAROLD. It's absolutely hateful.

ALAN. (*Rises.*) Hank, leave with me.

HANK. You don't understand, Alan. I can't. You can . . . but I can't.

ALAN. Why, Hank? Why can't you?

LARRY. (*To* HANK.) It he doesn't understand, why don't you explain it to him?

MICHAEL. *I'll* explain it.

HAROLD. I had a feeling you might.

MICHAEL. (*Puts phone on sofa.*) Although I doubt that it'll make any difference. That type refuses to understand that which they do not wish to accept. They reject certain facts. And Alan is decidedly from The Ostrich School of Reality. (*A beat.*) Alan . . . Larry and Hank are lovers. Not just roommates, *bed*-mates. *Lovers*.

ALAN. Michael! (*Turns away.*)

MICHAEL. No man's still got a *roommate* when he's over thirty years old. If they're not lovers, they're sisters.

(ALAN *sits Down Left chair.*)

LARRY. Hank is the one who's over thirty.

MICHAEL. (*Crosses to Center.*) Well, you're pushing it!

ALAN. . . . Hank?

HANK. (*Turns to* ALAN.) Yes, Alan. Larry is my lover.

ALAN. But you're married.

(MICHAEL, LARRY, EMORY, *and the* COWBOY *are sent into instant gales of laughter.*)

HAROLD. I think you said the wrong thing.

MICHAEL. Don't you love that quaint little idea?—if **a** man is married, then he is automatically heterosexual. (*A beat.*) Alan—Hank swings both ways—with a decided preference. (*A beat.*) Now. Who makes the first call? Emory?

EMORY. You go, Bernard.

BERNARD. I don't want to.

EMORY. I don't want to either. I don't want to at all.

DONALD. (*To himself.*) There are no accidents.

MICHAEL. Then, may I say, on your way home I hope you *will* yourself over an embankment.

EMORY. (*To* BERNARD.) Go on. Call up Peter Dahlbeck. That's who you'd like to call, isn't it?

MICHAEL. (*Crosses to* EMORY *above sofa.*) Who is Peter Dahlbeck?

EMORY. The boy in Detroit whose family Bernard's mother has been a laundress for since he was a pickaninny.

BERNARD. I worked for them too—after school and every summer.

EMORY. It's always been a large order of Hero Worship.

BERNARD. I think I've loved him all my life. But he never knew I was alive. Besides, he's straight.

COWBOY. So nothing ever happened between you?

EMORY. Oh, they finally made it—in the pool house one night after a drunken swimming party.

LARRY. With the right wine and the right music there're damn few that aren't curious.

MICHAEL. (*To* DONALD.) Sounds like there's a lot of Lady Chatterley in Mr. Dahlbeck, wouldn't you say, Donald?

DONALD. I've never been an O'Hara fan myself.

BERNARD. . . . And afterwards, we went swimming in the nude in the dark with only the moon reflecting on the water.

DONALD. Nor Thomas Merton.

BERNARD. It was beautiful.

MICHAEL. How romantic. And then the next morning you took him his coffée and alka-seltzer on a tray.

BERNARD. It was in the afternoon. I remember I was worried sick all morning about having to face him. But he pretended like nothing at all had happened.

MICHAEL. (*Looks at* DONALD.) Christ, he must have been so drunk he didn't remember a thing.

BERNARD. Yeah. I was sure relieved.

MICHAEL. Odd how that works. (*Put phone on coffee table.*) And now, for ten points, get that liar on the phone. (*A beat.* BERNARD *picks up the phone, dials.*)

LARRY. You *know* the number?

BERNARD. Sure. He's back in Grosse Pointe, living at home. He just got separated from his third wife. (ALL *watch* BERNARD *as he puts the receiver to his ear, waits. A beat. He hangs up quickly.*)

EMORY. D.A. or B.Y.?

COWBOY. What?

EMORY. D.A. or B.Y. That's operator lingo. It means— "Doesn't Answer" or "Busy."

MICHAEL. He didn't even give it time to find out. (*Coaxing.*) Go ahead, Bernard. Pick up the phone and dial. You'll think of something.—You know you want to call him. You know that, don't you? Well,—go ahead. (BERNARD *starts dialing.*) Your curiosity has got the best of you now. So . . . go on, call him.

(BERNARD *lets it ring this time.*)

HAROLD. Hateful.

BERNARD. . . . Hello?

MICHAEL. One point. (*He efficiently takes note on the pad.*)

(HANK *crosses to the Onstage landing area.*)

BERNARD. Who's speaking? Oh . . . Mrs. Dahlbeck.

MICHAEL. (*Taking note.*) One point.

BERNARD. . . . It's Bernard.—Francine's boy.

EMORY. *Son,* not *boy.*

BERNARD. . . . How are you?—Good. Good. Oh, just fine, thank you.—Mrs. Dahlbeck, is . . . Peter—at home?—Oh. Oh, I see.

MICHAEL. (*Crosses up to desk and back to* BERNARD.) Shhhhiiii . . .

BERNARD. . . . Oh, no. No, it's nothing important. I just wanted to . . . to tell him . . . that . . . to tell him I . . .

MICHAEL. (*Prompting flatly.*) I love him. That I've always loved him.

BERNARD. . . . that I was sorry to hear about him and his wife.

MICHAEL. No points! (*Crosses above sofa.*)

BERNARD. . . . My mother wrote me.—Yes. It is. It really is.—Well. Would you just tell him I called and said . . . that I was—just—very, very sorry to hear and I . . . hope—they can get everything straightened out.— Yes. Yes. Well, good night.—Goodbye.

(*He hangs up slowly.* MICHAEL *draws a definite line across his pad, makes a definite period.*)

MICHAEL. Two points total. Terrible. Next!

EMORY. Are you all right, Bernard?

BERNARD. (*Almost to himself.*) Why did I call? Why did I do that?

LARRY. (*To* BERNARD.) Where was he?

BERNARD. Out on a date. (*Hangs up phone and goes to Left table.*)

MICHAEL. Come on, Emory. Punch in. (*Turns phone toward* EMORY.)

(DONALD *rises, goes to high stool and sits.* EMORY *picks up the phone, dials information.* LARRY *rises and crosses Right side of sofa. A beat.*)

EMORY. Could I have the number, please—in the Bronx
—for a Delbert Botts.

LARRY. *A* Delbert Botts! How many can there be! (*Sits sofa.*)

BERNARD. Oh, I wish I hadn't called now.

EMORY. . . . No, the residence number, please. (*Grabs pencil from* MICHAEL'S *hand. He writes on the white, plastic phonecase. Into phone.*) . . . Thank you. (*And he indignantly slams down the receiver.*) I do wish information would stop calling me, "Ma'am"!

MICHAEL. By all means, scribble all over the telephone. (*He snatches the pencil from* EMORY'S *hands.*)

EMORY. It comes off with a little spit. (*Picks up his drink from coffee table.*)

MICHAEL. (*To* ALAN.) Like a lot of things.

LARRY. Who the hell is Delbert Botts?

EMORY. The one person I have always loved. (*To* MICHAEL.) That's who you said to call, isn't it?

MICHAEL. That's right, Emory board.

LARRY. How could you love anybody with a name like that?

MICHAEL. Yes, Emory, you couldn't love anybody with a name like that. It wouldn't look good on a place card. Isn't that right, Alan? (ALAN *is silent.*)

EMORY. I admit his name is not so good—but he is absolutely beautiful.—At least, he was when I was in high school. Of course, I haven't seen him since and he was about seven years older than I even then.

MICHAEL. (*Goes to bar, pours gin.*) Christ, you better call him quick before he dies.

EMORY. I've loved him ever since the first day I laid eyes on him which was when I was in the fifth grade and he was a senior.—Then, he went away to college and by the time he got out *I* was in high school, and he had become a dentist.

MICHAEL. (*With incredulous disgust.*) *A dentist!* (*Crosses above sofa with drink, leaving pad and pencil on bar.*)

EMORY. Yes. Delbert Botts, D.D.S. And he opened his office in a bank building.

(*Gives empty glass to* LARRY, *who hands it to* DONALD, *who refills it from martini pitcher.*)

HAROLD. And you went and had every tooth in your head pulled out, right?

EMORY. No. I just had my teeth cleaned, that's all. (*Gets his drink handed back.*)

(DONALD *decides to make a scotch for* ALAN.)

BERNARD. (*To himself.*) Oh, I shouldn't have called.

MICHAEL. (*To* BERNARD.) Will you shut-up, Bernard! And take your boring, sleep-making icks somewhere else. *Go!*

(BERNARD *takes the red wine bottle and glass and moves to the desk via above stair passage.* MICHAEL *crosses to Center.*)

EMORY. I remember I looked right into his eyes the whole time and I kept wanting to bite his fingers.

HAROLD. Well, it's absolutely mind boggling.

(DONALD *takes* ALAN *a scotch.*)

MICHAEL. Phyllis Phallic.

HAROLD. It absolutely boggles the mind.

(ALAN *takes the drink.*)

MICHAEL. (*Re:* DONALD's *action.*) Sara Samaritan.

(DONALD, *with his own drink, sits on landing.*)

EMORY. . . . I told him I was having my teeth cleaned

for the Junior-Senior Prom for which I was in charge of decorations. I told him it was a celestial theme and I was cutting stars out of tin foil and making clouds out of chicken wire and angel's hair. (*A beat.*) He couldn't have been less impressed.

COWBOY. I got angel's hair down my shirt once at Christmastime. Gosh, did it itch!

EMORY. . . . I told him I was going to burn incense in pots so that white fog would hover over the dance floor and it would look like heaven—just like I'd seen it in a Rita Hayworth movie.—I can't remember the title.

MICHAEL. The picture was called "Down To Earth." Any *kid* knows that.

COWBOY. . . . And it made little tiny cuts in the creases of my fingers. Man, did they sting! It would be terrible if you got that stuff in your . . . I'll be quiet.

(MICHAEL *goes to bar, leaves glass and picks up pad and pencil.*)

EMORY. He was engaged to this stupid-ass girl named Loraine whose mother was truly Supercunt.

MICHAEL. Don't digress. (*Crosses above sofa.*)

EMORY. Well, anyway, I was a wreck. I mean a total mess. I couldn't eat, sleep, stand up, sit down, *nothing*. I could hardly cut out silver stars or finish the clouds for the Prom. So I called him on the telephone and asked if I could see him alone.

HAROLD. Clearly not the coolest of moves.

EMORY. He said okay and told me to come by his house.—I was so nervous this time—my hands were shaking and my voice was unsteady. I couldn't look at him— I just stared straight in space and blurted out why I'd come.—I told him . . . I wanted him to be my friend. I said that I never knew anyone who I could talk to and tell everything to and trust. I asked him if he would be my friend.

COWBOY. You poor bastard.

MICHAEL. SHHHHHH!

BERNARD. What'd he say? (*Crossing to pillar Center with wine glass.*)

EMORY. He said he would be glad to be my friend. And anytime I ever wanted to see him or call him—to just call him and he'd see me. And he shook my trembling wet hand and I left on a cloud.

MICHAEL. One of the ones you made yourself.

EMORY. And the next day I went out and bought him a gold-plated cigarette lighter and had his initials mono-grammed on it and wrote a card that said, "From your friend, Emory."

HAROLD. Seventeen years old and already big with the gifts.

COWBOY. Yeah. And cards too.

EMORY. . . . And then the night of the Prom I found out.

BERNARD. Found out what?

EMORY. I heard two girls I knew giggling together. They were standing behind some god-damn corrugated card-board Greek columns I had borrowed from a department store and had draped with yards and yards of god-damn cheesecloth. Oh, Mary, it takes a fairy to make something pretty.

MICHAEL. *Don't digress.*

EMORY. This girl who was telling the story said she had heard it from her mother—and her mother had heard it from Loraine's mother. You see, Loraine and her mother were not beside the point. Obviously, Del had told Loraine about my calling and about the gift. (*A beat.*) Pretty soon everybody at the dance had heard about it and they were all laughing and making jokes. Everybody knew I had a crush on Doctor Delbert Botts and that I had asked him to be my friend. (*A beat.*) What they didn't know was that I *loved* him. And that I would go on loving him years after they had all forgotten my funny secret.

(*Pause.*)

HAROLD. Well, I for one, need an insulin injection.

MICHAEL. *Call him.*

BERNARD. (*Takes glass to desk and goes to* EMORY.) Don't, Emory.

MICHAEL. Since when are you telling him what to do!

EMORY. (*To* BERNARD.) What do I care—I'm pissed! I'll do anything. Three times.

BERNARD. Don't. *Please!* (*Squats Left of* EMORY.)

MICHAEL. I said call him.

BERNARD. Don't! You'll be sorry. Take my word for it.

EMORY. What have I got to lose?

BERNARD. Your dignity. That's what you've got to lose.

MICHAEL. (*Crosses to Left table and deposits pad and pencil.*) Well, *that's* a knee-slapper! I love *your* telling *him* about dignity when you allow him to degrade you constantly by Uncle Tom-ing you to death.

BERNARD. (*Rises and crosses to Center.*) *He* can do it, Michael. *I* can do it. But *you can't* do it.

MICHAEL. Isn't that discrimination?

BERNARD. I don't like it from him and I don't like it from me—but I do it to myself and I let him do it. I let him do it because it's the only thing that, to him, makes him my equal. We both got the short end of the stick—but I got a hell of a lot more than he did and he knows it. So, I let him Uncle Tom me just so he can tell himself he's not a complete loser.

MICHAEL. How very considerate.

BERNARD. It's his defense. You have your defense, Michael. But it's indescribable.

(EMORY *quietly licks his finger and begins to rub the number off the telephone case.*)

MICHAEL. (*To* BERNARD.) Y'all want to hear a little polite parlor jest from the liberal Deep South?—Do you know why *Nigras* have such big lips? Because they're always going, "p-p-p-p-a-a-a-h!"

(The labial noise is exasperating with lazy disgust. BER-
NARD *sits on second step.)*

DONALD. Christ, Michael!

MICHAEL. I can do without your god-damn spit all over
my telephone, you nellie coward.

(Grabs phone from EMORY *but Emory manages to keep it
from the tug of war.)*

EMORY. I may be nellie, but I'm no coward. (MICHAEL
*lets go of phone and goes Up Right corner to compose
himself. Starts to dial.)* Bernard, forgive me. I'm sorry. I
won't ever say those things to you again. (BERNARD *rises
and goes to desk and wine.)* B.Y.

MICHAEL. *(Crosses above sofa.)* It's busy?

EMORY. *(Nods.)* Loraine is probably talking to her
mother. Oh, yes, Delbert married Loraine.

MICHAEL. I'm sorry, you'll have to forfeit your turn.
We can't wait.

(He takes the phone from EMORY'S *lap and puts it in*
LARRY'S *lap.* LARRY *takes phone and starts to dial.)*

HAROLD. *(To* LARRY.) Well, you're not wasting any
time.

HANK. Who are you calling?

LARRY. Charlie.

*(*EMORY *jerks the phone out of* LARRY'S *hands.)*

EMORY. I refuse to forfeit my turn! It's *my turn* and
I'm taking it! *(Rises, backs Up into* MICHAEL'S *arms
with phone.)*

MICHAEL. That's the spirit, Emory! *Hit that iceberg—
don't miss it! Hit it! God-damnit!* I want a smash of a
finale! (MICHAEL *pushes* EMORY *to floor between ottoman and coffee table.)*

EMORY. Oh, God, I'm drunk.

MICHAEL. A falling-down-drunk-nellie-queen.

HAROLD. Well, that's the pot calling the kettle beige!

MICHAEL. (*Snapping; to* HAROLD.) *I am not drunk!* You cannot tell that I am drunk!—Donald! I'm not drunk! Am I!

DONALD. *I'm* drunk. '

EMORY. So am I. I am a *major drunk.*

MICHAEL. (*To* EMORY.) Shut up and dial! (*Goes to Left table for pad and pencil.*)

EMORY. (*Dialing.*) I am a major drunk of this or any other season.

DONALD. (*To* MICHAEL.) Don't you mean, shut up and *deal?*

EMORY. . . . It's ringing. It is no longer B.Y.—Hello?

MICHAEL. (*Taking note.*) One point.

EMORY. . . . Who's speaking? Who? . . . Doctor Delbert Botts?

MICHAEL. Two points.

EMORY. Oh, Del, is this really you?—Oh, nobody. You don't know me. You wouldn't remember me. I'm . . . just a friend. A falling-down drunken friend. Hello? Hello? Hello? (*He lowers the receiver.*) He hung up. (EMORY *hangs up the telephone.*)

MICHAEL. Three points total. You're winning.

EMORY. He said I must have the wrong party.

(BERNARD *exits kitchen Up Center.*)

HAROLD. (*Rises.*) He's right. We have the wrong party. We should be somewhere else.

EMORY. (*Rises, taking drink from coffee table, going to* HAROLD.) It's your party, Harold. Aren't you having a good time?

HAROLD. Simply fabulous. And what about you? Are you having a good time, Emory? Are you having as good a time as you thought you would? (*Puts* EMORY *in Down Right chair.*)

(LARRY *takes the phone.*)

MICHAEL. If you're bored, Harold, we could sing Happy Birthday again—to the tune of Havah Nagelah.

HAROLD. Not for all the tea in Mexico. (*Crosses Up Center to desk where he lights up a cigarette.*)

(LARRY *starts to dial.*)

HANK. My turn now. (*Crossing to* LARRY.)

LARRY. It's my turn to call Charlie.

HANK. No. Let me.

LARRY. Are *you* going to call Charlie?

MICHAEL. (*Crosses to Left of steps.*) The score is three to two. Emory's favor.

ALAN. Don't, Hank. Don't you see—Bernard was right.

HANK. (*Firmly to* ALAN.) I want to. (*He holds out his hand for the phone.*) Larry?

LARRY. (*Gives him the phone.*) Be my eager guest.

COWBOY. (*To* LARRY.) Is he going to call Charlie for you?

(HANK *starts to dial as he sits on sofa.* HAROLD *comes to bar.*)

LARRY. Charlie is all the people I cheat on Hank with.

DONALD. With whom I cheat on Hank.

MICHAEL. The butcher, the baker, the candlestick maker.

LARRY. Right! I love 'em all. And what Hank refuses to understand—is that I've got to *have* 'em all. I am *not* the marrying kind, and I never will be.

HAROLD. Gypsy feet. (*Crosses to Right end sofa.*)

LARRY. (*Step in to* HANK.) Who are you calling?

MICHAEL. Jealous?

LARRY. Curious as hell!

MICHAEL. And a little jealous too.

LARRY. Who are you calling?

MICHAEL. Did it ever occur to you that Hank might be doing the same thing behind your back that you do behind his?

LARRY. I wish to Christ he would. It'd make life a hell of a lot easier. Who are you calling? (*Sits ottoman.*)

HAROLD. Whoever it is, they're not sitting on top of the telephone. (*Sits sofa Right end.*)

HANK. Hello?

COWBOY. They must have been in the tub.

MICHAEL. (*Snaps at* COWBOY.) Eighty-six! (*Crossing above sofa.* BERNARD *enters, uncorking another bottle of wine and sits on desk. Taking note.*) One point.

HANK. . . . I'd like to leave a message.

MICHAEL. Not in. One point.

HANK. Would you say that Hank called.—Yes, it is. Oh, good evening, how are you?

LARRY. Who the hell *is* that? (*Grabs for phone but* HANK *keeps phone and transfers it to other ear.*)

HANK. . . . Yes, that's right—the message is for my roommate, Larry. Just say that I called and . . .

LARRY. It's our answering service! (*Rising and going Up Center to pillar.*)

HANK. . . . and said . . . I love you.

MICHAEL. (*Crosses to Right end sofa.*) *Five points!* You said it! You get five god-damn points for saying it!

ALAN. (*Rises and crosses in.*) Hank! . . . Are you crazy?

HANK. (*Into phone.*) . . . No. You didn't hear me incorrectly. That's what I said. The message is for Larry and it's from me, Hank, and it is just as I said—*I . . . love . . . you.* Thanks. (*He hangs up and rises.*)

MICHAEL. Seven points total! Hank, you're ahead, baby. You're way, way ahead of everybody!

ALAN. Why, Hank? Why did you do that?

HANK. Because I do love him. And I don't care who knows it.

ALAN. Don't say that.

HANK. Why not? It's the truth.

ALAN. I can't believe you.

HANK. (*Crossing to* ALAN.) I left my wife and family for Larry.

ALAN. I'm really not interested in hearing about it. (*Turns back to chair.*)

MICHAEL. Sure you are. Go ahead, Hankola, tell him all about it.

ALAN. No! I don't want to hear it. It's disgusting! (*Sits in same chair.*)

HANK. Some men do it for another woman.

ALAN. Well, I could understand *that*. That's *normal*.

HANK. It just doesn't always work out that way. No matter how you might want it to. And God knows, Alan, nobody ever wanted it more than I did. I really and truly felt that I was in love with my wife when I married her. It wasn't altogether my trying to prove something to myself. I did love her and she loved me. But . . . there was always that something there.

DONALD. You mean your attraction to your own sex.

HANK. Yes.

ALAN. Always?

HANK. I don't know. I suppose so. (*Goes to Left table.*)

EMORY. I've known what I was since I was four years old.

MICHAEL. Everybody's always known it about *you*, Emory.

DONALD. (*Rises and sits stool at door.*) I've always known it about myself too.

HANK. (*Crosses to Left of steps.*) I don't know when it was that I started admitting it to myself. For so long I either labeled it something else or denied it completely.

MICHAEL. Christ-was-I-drunk-last-night.

HANK. And then there came a time when I just couldn't lie to myself any more . . . I thought about it but I never did anything about it.—I think the first time was during my wife's last pregnancy. We lived near Hartford—in the country. She and the kids still live there.—Well, anyway, there was a teachers' meeting here in New York. She didn't feel up to the trip and I came alone. And that day on the train I began to think about it and think about it and think about it. I thought of nothing else the whole trip. And within fifteen minutes after I had arrived I had picked up a guy in the men's room of Grand Central Station.

ALAN. (*Quietly.*) Jesus.

HANK. I'd never done anything like that in my life and I was scared to death. But he turned out to be a nice fellow. I've never seen him again and it's funny I can't even remember his name any more. (*A beat.*) Anyway. After that, it got easier.

HAROLD. Practice makes perfect.

HANK. And then . . . sometime later . . . not very long after, Larry was in Hartford and we met at a party my wife and I had gone in town for.

EMORY. And your real troubles began.

HANK. That was two years ago.

LARRY. Why am I always the god-damn villain in the piece! If I'm not thought of as a happy home wrecker, I'm an impossible son-of-a-bitch to live with!

HAROLD. Guilt turns to hostility. Isn't that right, Michael?

MICHAEL. Go stick your tweezers in your cheek.

LARRY. I'm fed up to the teeth with everybody feeling so god-damn sorry for poor shat-upon Hank.

EMORY. Aw, Larry, everybody knows you're Frida Fickle.

LARRY. (*Rises.*) I've never made any promises and I never intend to. It's my right to lead my sex life without answering to *anybody*—Hank included!—And if those terms are not acceptable, then we must not live together.— Numerous relations is a part of the way I am! (*Crosses to bar.*)

(MICHAEL *rises and takes Center Stage.*)

EMORY. You don't have to be gay to be a wanton.

LARRY. By the way I am, I don't mean being gay—I mean my sexual appetite. And I don't think of myself as a wanton. Emory, you are the most promiscuous person I know. (*Crosses Up Center.*)

EMORY. I am not promiscuous at all!

MICHAEL. (*Crosses to bar to pour another gin.*) Not by choice, by design. Why would anybody want to go to bed with a flaming little sissy like you?

BERNARD. Michael! (*Crosses in to pillar with wine bottle and glass.*)

MICHAEL. (*To* EMORY.) Who'd make a pass at you?— I'll tell you who—nobody. Except maybe some fugitive from the Braille Institute.

BERNARD. (*To* EMORY.) Why do you let him talk to you that way?

HAROLD. Physical beauty is not everything.

MICHAEL. Thank you, Quasimodo. (*Crossing above sofa with drink and pad.*)

LARRY. (*Crosses to Center.*) What do you think it's like living with the god-damn gestapo! I can't breathe without getting the third degree!

MICHAEL. Larry, it's your turn to call. (*Sits on sofa back.*)

LARRY. (*Steps to Right.*) I can't take all that let's-be-faithful-and-never-look-at-another-person-routine. It just doesn't work.—If you want to promise that, fine. Then do it and stick to it. But if you *have* to promise it—as far as I'm concerned—nothing finishes a relationship faster. (*Crosses to steps to* HANK.)

HAROLD. Give me librium or give me meth.

BERNARD. (*Intoxicated now.*) Yeah, freedom, baby! Freedom!

LARRY. (*Crosses Center.*) You gotta have it! It can't work any other way. And the ones who swear their undying fidelity are lying. Most of them, anyway—ninety percent of them. They cheat on each other constantly and lie through their teeth. I'm sorry, I can't be like that and it drives Hank up the wall.

HANK. There is that ten percent.

LARRY. The only way it stands a chance is with some sort of an understanding.

HANK. I've tried to go along with that.

LARRY. Aw, *come on!*

HANK. I agreed to an agreement.

LARRY. Your agreement.

MICHAEL. What agreement? (*Stands up.*)

LARRY. A menage.

HAROLD. The lover's agreement.

LARRY. Look, I know a lot of people think it's the answer. They don't consider it cheating. But it's not my style.

HANK. Well, *I* certainly didn't want it.

LARRY. Then who suggested it?

HANK. It was a compromise.

LARRY. Exactly.

HANK. And you agreed.

LARRY. I didn't agree to anything. You agreed to your own proposal and *informed me* that I agreed.

(HANK *goes to sofa and sits.*)

COWBOY. I don't understand. What's a me . . . menaa . . .

MICHAEL. A menage a trois, baby. Two's company—three's a menage.

HANK. Well, it works for some.

LARRY. Well, I'm not one for group therapy. I'm sorry, I can't relate to anyone or anything that way. I'm old-fashioned—I like 'em all, but I like 'em one at a time!

MICHAEL. (*To* LARRY.) Did you like Donald as a single side attraction?

(*Pause.* DONALD *rises, crosses to Right end sofa.*)

LARRY. Yes. I did.

DONALD. So did I, Larry.

LARRY. (*To* DONALD *re:* MICHAEL.) Did you tell him?
DONALD. No.

MICHAEL. (*Crosses to* LARRY.) It was perfectly obvious from the moment you walked in the door. What was this big song and dance about having seen each other but never having met?

DONALD. It was true. We saw each other in the baths and went to bed together but we never spoke a word and never knew each other's names.

EMORY. You had better luck than I do. If I don't get arrested, my trick announces upon departure that he's been exposed to hepatitis!

MICHAEL. In spring a young man's fancy turns to a fancy youny man. (*Goes to Left table and puts drink, pad and pencil down.*)

LARRY. (*Crosses to* HANK.) Don't look at me like that. You've been playing footsie with the Blue Book all night.

DONALD. I think he only wanted to show you what's good for the gander is good for the gander.

HANK. That's right.

(DONALD *returns to his stool.*)

LARRY. (*To* HANK.) I suppose you'd like the three of us to have a go at it.

HANK. At least it'd be together.

LARRY. That point eludes me. (*Crosses Left of steps.*)

HANK. What kind of an understanding do you *want!*

LARRY. Respect—for each other's freedom. With no need to lie or pretend. (*Crosses to* HANK *and kneels.*) In my own way, Hank, I love you, but you've got to understand that even though I do want to go on living with you, sometimes there may be others. I don't want to flaunt it in your face. If it happens I know I'll never mention it. But if you ask me, I'll tell you. I don't want to hurt you but I won't lie to you if you want to know anything about me.

BERNARD. He gets points.

MICHAEL. What?

BERNARD. He said it—he said, "I love you," to Hank—he ge's the bonus.

MICHAEL. He didn't call him..

DONALD. He called him. He just didn't use the telephone.

MICHAEL. Then he doesn't get any points.

BERNARD. He gets five points!

MICHAEL. He didn't use the telephone—he doesn't get a god-damn thing!

(LARRY *goes to the phone, picks up the receiver, looks at the number of the second line, dials. A beat. The PHONE rings.*)

LARRY. It's for you, Hank. Why don't you take it upstairs?

(*The phone continues to ring.* HANK *gets up, goes up the stairs to the bedroom. Pause. He presses the second line button, picks up the receiver.* EVERYONE *downstairs is silent.*)

HANK. Hello?

BERNARD. One point.

LARRY. Hello, Hank.

BERNARD. Two points.

LARRY. . . . This is Larry.

BERNARD. Two more points!

LARRY. . . . For what it's worth, I love you.

BERNARD. Five points bonus!

HANK. I'll . . . I'll try.

LARRY. I will too. (*He hangs up.* HANK *hangs up.*)

BERNARD. That's ten points total! (*Rises and comes down steps to Up Center.*)

EMORY. Larry's the winner! (*Rises and stretches.*)

(DONALD *rises and pulls high stool to right of desk and*

gets up Right Center. COWBOY *rises and puts cushion under bar and sits Right end of sofa.* EMORY *continues via below coffee table to stairs.*)

HAROLD. (*Rises.*) Well, that wasn't as much fun as I thought it would be.

(ALAN *rises and crosses to Left table.*)

MICHAEL. THE GAME ISN'T OVER YET! (*Meets* EMORY *and pushes him Up Center.*) —Your turn, Alan. (*Goes to* ALAN.) PICK UP THE PHONE, BUSTER! (*Grabs* ALAN'S *arm and swings him to below ottoman.*)

EMORY. (*Crosses to* MICHAEL.) Michael, don't!

MICHAEL. STAY OUT OF THIS! (*Pushes* EMORY *Left.*)

EMORY. You don't have to, Alan. You don't have to.

ALAN. Emory . . . I'm sorry for what I did before.

(*A beat.*)

EMORY. . . . Oh, forget it.

MICHAEL. Forgive us our trespasses. Christ, now you're both joined at the goddamn hip! (*Forcing* EMORY *to sit in Down Left chair by crossing in on* EMORY.) You can decorate his home, Emory—and he can get you out of jail the next time he's arrested on a morals charge. (MICHAEL *turns to* ALAN *as* ALAN *turns Upstage. A beat.*) Who are you going to call, Alan? (*No response.*) Can't remember anyone? Well, maybe you need a minute to think. Is that it? (*No response.* ALAN *sits ottoman.*)

HAROLD. (*Crosses to Left table.*) I believe this will be the final round.

COWBOY. Michael, aren't you going to call anyone?

HAROLD. How could he?—He's never loved anyone.

MICHAEL. (*Sings the classic vaudeville walk-off to* HAROLD.)

> "No matter how you figger,
> It's tough to be a nigger,

But it's tougher
To be a Jeeeew-ooouu-oo!"
> (*Turns to* HAROLD *and flicks* HAROLD'*s
> scarf.*)

DONALD. My God, Michael, you're a charming host.

HAROLD. Michael doesn't have charm, Donald. Michael has counter-charm.

(LARRY *crosses to the stairs.*)

MICHAEL. Going somewhere?

LARRY. (*He stops, turns to* MICHAEL.) Yes. Excuse me.

MICHAEL. You're going to miss the end of the game.

LARRY. (*Pauses on stairs.*) You can tell me how it comes out.

MICHAEL. I never reveal an ending. And no one will be re-seated during the climactic revelation.

LARRY. With any luck I won't be back until it's all over. (*He turns, continues up the stairs.* LARRY *exits Left from second floor escape.*)

MICHAEL. (*Crosses to* ALAN.) What do you suppose is going on up there? Hmmm, Alan? What do you imagine Larry and Hank are doing? Hmmmmm? Shooting marbles?

EMORY. Whatever they're doing, they're not hurting anyone.

HAROLD. And they're minding their own business.

MICHAEL. (*Crosses to* HAROLD.) And you mind yours, Harold. I'm warning you!

(*A beat.*)

HAROLD. (*Coolly.*) Are you now? Are you warning *me? Me?* I'm Harold. I'm the one person you don't warn, Michael. Because you and I are a match.—And we tread very softly with each other because we both play each other's game too well. Oh, I know this game you're playing. I know it very well. And I *play* it very well.—You play it very well too. But you know what? I'm the only one that's better at it than you are. I can beat you at it. So don't push me. I'm warning *you*.

(*A beat.* MICHAEL *starts to laugh.*)

MICHAEL. You're funny, Hallie. A laff-riot. Isn't he funny, Alan? Or, as you might say, isn't he amusing? He's an amusing faggot, isn't he? Or, as you might say, freak. —That's what you called Emory, wasn't it? A freak? A pansy? My, what an antiquated vocabulary you have. I'm surprised you didn't say sodomite or pedarist. (*A beat.*) You'd better let me bring you up to date.—Now it's not so new but it might be new to you— (*A beat.*) Have you heard the term, "closet queen"? Do you know what that means? Do you know what it means to be "in the closet"?

(BERNARD *goes to front of landing and collapses to floor.*)

EMORY. Don't, Michael. It won't help anything to explain what it means.

MICHAEL. (*Crosses to* EMORY.) He already knows. He knows very, very well what a closet queen is. Don't you, Alan?

ALAN. Michael, if you are insinuating that I am homosexual, I can only say that you are mistaken.

MICHAEL. Am I? (*A beat.*) What about Justin Stuart?

ALAN. . . . What about . . . Justin Stuart?

MICHAEL. (*Crosses to phone above sofa.*) You were in love with him, that's what about him. And *that* is who you are going to call. (*Slams phone from sofa Center to Left end.*)

ALAN. Justin and I were very good friends. That is all. Unfortunately, we had a parting of the ways and that was the end of the friendship. We have not spoken for years. I most certainly will not call him now. (*Rises and crosses to Left end of sofa.*)

MICHAEL. (*Crosses Right end sofa.*) According to Justin, the friendship was quite passionate.

ALAN. What do you mean?

MICHAEL. I mean that you slept with him in college. Several times.

ALAN. That's not true!

MICHAEL. Several times. Once that's youth. Twice, a phase maybe. Several times, *you like it!*

ALAN. That's NOT TRUE!

MICHAEL. Yes, it is true. Because Justin Stuart *is* homosexual. He comes to New York on occasion. He calls me. I've taken him to parties. Larry's "had" him once. *I* have slept with Justin. And he has told me all about *you.*

ALAN. Then he told you a lie.

MICHAEL. You were obsessed with Justin. That's all you talked about morning, noon, and night. You started doing it about Hank upstairs tonight.—What an attractive fellow he is and all that transparent crap.

ALAN. He *is* an attractive fellow. What's wrong with saying so?

MICHAEL. Would you like to join him and Larry right now?

ALAN. I said he was attractive. That's all.

MICHAEL. How many times do you have to say it? How many times did you have to say it about Justin?—what a good tennis player he was—what a good dancer he was— what a good body he had—what good taste he had—how bright he was—how *amusing* he was—how the girls were all mad for him—what close friends you were. (*Crosses Right end coffee table.*)

ALAN. We were very close . . . very good friends. *That's all!* (*Crosses to* MICHAEL.)

MICHAEL. It was *obvious*—and when you did it around *Fran* it was downright embarrassing. Even she must have had her doubts about you.

ALAN. *Justin . . . lied.* If he told you that, he lied. It is a lie. A vicious lie. He'd say anything about me now to get even. He could never get over the fact that *I* dropped *him*. But I had to. I had to because he told me about himself . . . he told me that he wanted me to be his lover.

And I told him that he made me sick . . . I told him I pitied him. (*Sits sofa.*)

MICHAEL. You ended the friendship, Alan, because you couldn't face the truth about yourself. (*Crosses to Left end sofa.*) You could go along, sleeping with Justin as long as he lied to himself and you lied to yourself and you both dated girls and labeled yourselves men and called yourselves just fond friends. But Justin finally had to be honest about the truth, and you couldn't take it. (MICHAEL *goes to the desk, and gets address book.*) You couldn't take it and so you destroyed the friendship and your friend along with it. (*Crosses to* ALAN.)

ALAN. No!

MICHAEL. Justin could never understand what he'd done wrong to make you drop him. He blamed himself.

ALAN. No!

MICHAEL. He did until he eventually found out who he was and what he was.

ALAN. No!

MICHAEL. But to this day, he still remembers the treatment—the scars he got from you. (*He puts address book in front of* ALAN *on coffee table.*)

ALAN. NO!

MICHAEL. Pick up this phone and call Justin. Call him and apologize and tell him what you should have told him twelve years ago.

(*He picks up the phone, shoves it at* ALAN.)

ALAN. NO! HE LIED! *NOT A WORD IS TRUE!*

MICHAEL. Call him! (ALAN *won't take it.*) All right then, *I'll dial!*

HAROLD. You're so helpful.

(MICHAEL *starts to dial.*)

ALAN. Give it to me. (*Clicking off dialing.* MICHAEL *hands* ALAN *the receiver.* ALAN *takes it, releases cradle button, starts to dial.* EVERYONE *is watching in silent attention.* ALAN *finishes dialing, lifts the receiver to his ear.*) . . . Hello?

MICHAEL. One point.

ALAN. . . . It's . . . it's Alan.

MICHAEL. Two points.

ALAN. . . . Yes, yes, it's *me.*

MICHAEL. Is it Justin?

ALAN. . . . You sound surprised.

MICHAEL. I should hope to think so—after twelve years! Two more points.

ALAN. No, I'm in New York. Yes. I won't explain now . . . I . . . I just called to tell you . . .

MICHAEL. THAT I LOVE YOU, GOD-DAMNIT! *I LOVE YOU!*

ALAN. I love you.

MICHAEL. FIVE POINTS BONUS. TEN POINTS TOTAL! JACKPOT!

ALAN. I love you and I beg you to forgive me.

MICHAEL. Give me that!. (*He snatches the phone from* ALAN.) Justin! Did you hear what that son-of-a-bitch said! (*A beat.* MICHAEL *is speechless for a moment.*) Fran. (*A beat.* MICHAEL *sits on sofa.*) Fran, of course, I expected it to be you! How are you? . . . Me too . . . Yes, he told me everything . . . Oh, don't thank *me, please!* I'll put him back on. My love to the kids.

(MICHAEL *lowers his hand with the receiver and* ALAN *takes the receiver as* MICHAEL *stares front.*)

ALAN. . . . Darling? I'll take the first plane I can get. —Yes. I'm sorry too. Yes . . . I love you very much. (*He hangs up, stands up, crosses to the door, stops. He turns around, surveys the* GROUP.) Thank you, Michael. (*He opens the door and exits.*)

(*Silence.* MICHAEL *brings hands to face and sinks face into seat of sofa.*)

COWBOY. Who won?

DONALD. It was a tie.

HAROLD. (HAROLD *crosses to* MICHAEL. *Calmly, coldly, clinically.*) Now it is my turn. And ready or not, Michael, here goes. (*A beat.*) You are a sad and pathetic man. You're a homosexual and you don't want to be. But there is nothing you can do to change it.—Not all your prayers to your God, not all the analysis you can buy in all the years you've got left to live. You may very well one day be able to know a heterosexual life if you want it desperately enough—if you pursue it with the fervor with which you annihilate—but you will always be homosexual as well. Always, Michael. Always. Until the day you die. (*He turns, goes toward* EMORY.) Oh, friends, thanks for the nifty party and the super gift. (*He looks toward the* COWBOY.) It's just what I needed. (EMORY *smiles.* HAROLD *spots* BERNARD *sitting on the floor, head bowed.*) . . . Bernard, thank you. (*No response. To* EMORY.) Will you get him home?

EMORY. Don't worry about her. I'll take care of everything.

(HAROLD *turns, passes* DONALD *who is sitting on steps and goes to Up Center.*)

HAROLD. Donald, good to see you.

DONALD. Good night, Harold. See you again sometime.

HAROLD. Yeah. How about a year from Shevuoth? (*Goes to desk chair and gathers gifts and goes to* COWBOY.) Come on, Tex. Let's go to my place. (*The* COWBOY *gets up.*) Are you good in bed?

COWBOY. Well . . . I'm not like the average hustler you'd meet. I try to show a little affection—it keeps me from feeling like such a whore.

(HAROLD *gives* COWBOY *the gifts.* COWBOY *takes gifts, goes to door and opens it.*)

HAROLD. (*Picks up his eye glasses from bar.*) Oh,
Michael . . . thanks for the laughs. Call you tomorrow.

(*No response.* HAROLD *and the* COWBOY *exit.*)

EMORY. Come on, Bernard. Time to go home.

(EMORY, *frail as he is, manages to pull* BERNARD'S *arm
around his neck, gets him on his feet.*)

BERNARD. (*Practically inaudible mumble.*) Why did I
call? Why?
EMORY. Oh, Mary, you're a heavy mother. (*Takes*
BERNARD *to Left end of sofa.*) Thank you, Michael. Good
night, Donald.
DONALD. Goodbye, Emory.
BERNARD. Why . . . (*As* EMORY *crosses to door with*
BERNARD.)
EMORY. It's all right, Bernard. Everything's all right.
I'm going to make you some coffee and everything's going
to be all right.

(EMORY *virtually carries* BERNARD *out.* DONALD *closes the
door.* MICHAEL *slides to floor and begins a low moan
that increases in volume—almost like a siren—to a
bloodcurdling shriek. He slams his open hands on
floor.*)

MICHAEL. (*In desperate panic.*) Donald! Donald!
DONALD! *DONALD!* (DONALD *puts down his drink,
rushes to* MICHAEL. MICHAEL *is now white with fear and
tears are bursting from his eyes. He begins to gasp his
words.*) Oh, no! No! What have I done! Oh, my God,
what have I done! (MICHAEL *starts to writhe.* DONALD
grabs him, cradles him in his arms.)
DONALD. Michael! Michael!
MICHAEL. (*Tears pouring forth.*) Oh, no! NO! It's be-
ginning! The anxiety! OH, NO! No! I feel it! I know it's

going to happen. Donald!! Donald! Don't leave. Please! Please! Oh, my God, what have I done! Oh Jesus, I can't handle it. I won't make it!

DONALD. (*Physically subduing him.*) Michael! Michael! Stop it! Stop it! I'll give you a Valium—I've got some in my pocket!

MICHAEL. (*Hysterical.*) No! No! Pills and alcohol— I'll die!

DONALD. I'm not going to give you the whole bottle! Come on, let go of me!

MICHAEL. (*Clutching him.*) *NO!*

DONALD. Let go of me long enough for me to get my hand in my pocket!

MICHAEL. Don't leave! (*As he loosens his grip he crumbles to the floor.*)

(MICHAEL *quiets a bit, as* DONALD *gets a pill from his pocket.*)

DONALD. Here. (*Putting pill in* MICHAEL'S. *hand as he pulls* MICHAEL'S *head and arms up from floor.*)

MICHAEL. (*Sobbing.*) I don't have any water to swallow it with!

DONALD. Well, if you'll wait one god-damn minute, I'll get you some! (*He goes to the bar, gets a glass of water.* MICHAEL *collapses, his head on the sofa seat.* DONALD *returns with glass.*) Your water, Your Majesty. (*A beat.* DONALD *puts glass in* MICHAEL'S *hand as he pulls* MICHAEL'S *head up.*) Michael, stop that god-damn crying and take this pill!

(MICHAEL *puts the pill into his mouth amid choking sobs, takes the water, washes it down, returns the glass to* DONALD *which* DONALD *returns to bar.*)

MICHAEL. (*Sitting on sofa.*) I'm like Ole Man River— tired of livin' and scared o' dyin'.

(DONALD *helps* MICHAEL *to sit sofa and also sits down.*
MICHAEL *collapses into his arms, sobbing.*)

DONALD. Shhhhh.   Shhhhhh.   Michael.   Shhhhhh.
Michael. Michael.

(DONALD *rocks him back and forth. He quiets.*)

MICHAEL. . . . If we . . . if we could just . . . learn
not to hate ourselves so much. That's it, you know. If we
could just not hate ourselves just quite so very very
much.

DONALD. Yes, I know. I know. (*A beat.*) Inconceivable
as it may be, you used to be worse than you are now.
Maybe with a lot more work you can help yourself some
more—if you try.

(MICHAEL *straightens up, dries his eyes in his handker-*
chief.)

MICHAEL. Who was it that used to always say, "You
show me a happy homosexual, and I'll show you a gay
corpse."

DONALD. I don't know. Who was it who always used to
say that?

MICHAEL. (*Pulls away so* DONALD'S *arm is free from*
him.) And how dare you come on with that holier-than-
thou attitude with me!—"A lot more work," "if I try,"
indeed! You've got a long row to hoe before you're perfect, you know.

DONALD. I never said I didn't.

MICHAEL. And while we're on the subject—I think
your analyst is a quack. (MICHAEL *blows his nose.*)

DONALD. Earlier you said he was a prick.

MICHAEL. That's right. He's a prick quack. Or a quack
prick, whichever you prefer.

(DONALD *gets up from the sofa, goes to bar and pours a*
brandy.)

DONALD. (*Heaving a sigh.*) Harold was right. You'll never change.

MICHAEL. Come back, Donald. Come back, Shane. (*Catching himself at a movie imitation.*)

DONALD. I'll come back when you have another anxiety attack.

MICHAEL. I need you. Just like Mickey Mouse needs Minnie Mouse—just like Donald Duck needs . . . Minnie Duck—Mickey needs Donnie.

DONALD. My name is Donald. I am called Donald. You must never call anyone called Donald, Donnie.

MICHAEL. (*Grabs his head, moans and rises, going Left of steps.*) Ohhhhh . . . icks! Icks! Terrible icks! Tomorrow is going to be "Bad Day at Black Rock." A day of nerves, nerves, and more nerves! (MICHAEL *surveys the room.*) Do you suppose there's any possibility of just burning this room? (*Goes to candles and puts them out.*)

(*A beat.*)

DONALD. Why do you think he stayed, Michael? Why do you think he took all of that from you?

MICHAEL. There are no accidents. He was begging to get killed. He begged for somebody to let him have it and he got what he wanted.

DONALD. He could have been telling the truth—Justin could have lied. (*Crossing to sofa.*)

MICHAEL. Who knows? What time is it?

DONALD. It seems like it's day after tomorrow. (*Sits sofa.*)

(MICHAEL *goes toward kitchen glancing Off Left to clock. He comes back to pillar and gets his raincoat.*)

MICHAEL. It's early. (*Leans wearily on pillar.*)

DONALD. What does life *hold?* Where're you going?

MICHAEL. The bedroom is occupado and I don't want to go to sleep anyway until I try to walk-off some of this booze. If I went to sleep like this, when I wake up they'd have to put me in a padded cell—not that that's where I don't belong. (*A beat.*) And there's a midnight mass at St. Malachy's that all the show people go to. I think I'll walk over there and catch it.

DONALD. (*Raises his glass.*) Well, pray for me.

MICHAEL. (*Indicates bedroom.*) Maybe they'll be gone by the time I get back.

DONALD. (*Rises and goes to bar.*) Well, *I* will be—just as soon as I knock off this bottle of brandy. (*Pours brandy to his snifter.*)

MICHAEL. Will I see you next Saturday?

DONALD. (*Turns to MICHAEL.*) Unless you have other plans. (MICHAEL *shakes his head "no."*) Michael, did he ever tell you why he was crying on the phone—what it was he *had* to tell you?

MICHAEL. No. It must have been that he'd left Fran.— Or maybe it was something else and he changed his mind.

DONALD. Maybe so. (*A beat.*) I wonder why he left her.

MICHAEL. (*Wearily.*) . . . As my father said to me when he died in my arms, "I don't understand any of it. I never did." (*A beat.* DONALD *goes to his stack of books, selects one, sits Down Right chair.*) Turn out the lights when you leave, will you?

(DONALD *nods.* MICHAEL *goes to the door, opens it and exits closing door behind him as:*)

LIGHTS FADE OUT

THE END

PROPERTY LIST

PRESET:

ON STAGE
  Buffet table on marks* (Left)
    On:
      2 candles in holders (practical dripless)
      White small box of matches
  Armless chair on marks (Down Left)
  Tall stool on marks (Center by Stairs)
  Short stool on marks (Right Center)
  Desk table (attached to wall)* (Up Right Center)
    On:
      Record player*
      10 45 rpm records
      White telephone with buttons
        (hold button and 4 or 5 line buttons)*
      Unopened package of cigarettes
      Small box of matches
      Magic bow
        (ribbon folded in loops which actor forms into a bow)*
      Small solid color shopping bag*
        In:
          Toothbrush in case
          Sandalwood soap box (soap inside not needed)
          "Control" hair spray can*
      Small pair of scissors
      Small dispenser of scotch tape
      Telephone address book with Stuart page written in
      Writing pad (approx. 5½" x 8½" unlined)
      2 sharpened pencils
  Desk chair (armless) (pushed under desk)
  Sofa on marks* (Right Center)
  Coffee table on marks*
    On:
      Wrapped box with silver framed photograph
      Pre-cut ribbon (to fit above box)
      Ash tray with felt bottom dampened (black plastic)
      Small box of safety matches
  Arm chair on marks (Down Right)
  Bar table on marks (attached to wall) (Right)
    Under:
      Wastebasket (black)
      Small pillow (black)

105

On:

    Open Beefeater's gin bottle (filled with water)
    Open vodka bottle (filled with water)
    Open vermouth bottle (filled with water)
    Capped club soda bottle (filled with water)* Canada Dry
    Capped quinine water bottle (filled with water)
    Corked brandy bottle (half-filled) (tea)
    Folded bar towel
    2 bottle openers
    Shot glass
    Small box of safety matches
    3 black plastic ash trays (with felt bottoms dampened)
    Cork screw

Bar table

  On:

    12 airline plastic glasses cocktail
    1 brandy snifter
    2 stem wine glasses
    Martini pitcher (empty)
    Water pitcher (filled with water)
    2 plastic water tumbler glasses

BEDROOM—2d level

  Bed (specially made) with bedspread and pillow

    Under:

      Special foot board piece (black)*

  Side table

    On:

      Kent-type comb
      Tan sweater folded

  Bench at foot of bed

    Under:

      Michael's shoes

  Arm chair

    On:

      Hairdryer (unwound cord)

  Small table

    On:

      Black telephone similar to downstairs phone
      Shoe mit (put on hand like glove to polish shoes)

OFF STAGE—*Right* (Bedroom 2d level—Bathroom)

  Chair
  Box of tissues

Plastic tumbler water glass with ¼ water
Donald's shirt folded (Navy blue)
Michael's trousers with belt, fly unzipped, hanky in back right pocket

OFF STAGE—*Left* (Bedroom 2d level) Behind sliding door*
  On a shelf or prop table—
    Red sweater folded (on bottom)
    Maroon sweater folded (on top)

OFF STAGE—*Right* (1st level)
  Airline bag with padding (small with handles gym-type)
  6 books (novels)
  Foil-covered casserole (Corning ware 2½ qt. size)
  Tissue-wrapped "Boardwalk" plaque
  Decorative sweater box (stretch ribbon around)
    (no unwrapping)
    In:
      Tan sweater and gift card (Hank)
      The above sweater in a plastic bag
  2 bottles of wine (practical—opened and drunk)
  Box wrapped decoratively but remains a box
    (so no unwrapping)
    In:
      "Bejeweled" kneepads (green with sequins H on 1 pad, B on other)
      Gift card (Bernard)
  Bakery cake box (empty)
    * *Black foot board used in Act II to mask bed.*
    Sliding panel used to mask when LARRY *exits to bedroom in Act II.*

OFF STAGE—*Left*—1st level
  Bud vase with 1 plastic red rose
  Scotch bottle (JB) filled with light tea with cap on loosely
  Ice bucket with ice*
  Cracked crab tray
    (Silver tray with styrofoam ice dip dish with yellow cotton crab claws meticulously cleaned in ice)
  Beer tub (cannister can painted black)* with lid loose
    In:
      Two "unpopped" lift-open beer cans
  2 wine glasses
  Trivet for casserole

Napkin holder with 10 paper napkins (white napkins)

7 white plates

Pot holder (black and white if possible)

2 pots of metal for dropping to floor for "CRASH" SOUND off ULC)

ON STAGE—*Behind Center Pillar*
  Michael's raincoat on hook

PERSONAL PROPS:
  DONALD—pipe
  HANK—pipe, wedding ring, package of cigarettes
  COWBOY—birthday card with wrist ribbon*
  HAROLD—cigarette "joints" (Pall Mall cigarettes somewhat dried out so that one end is slightly emptied and the paper twisted)*
  A Mild Pipe Tobacco for Above Pipes

BOYS IN THE BAND PROPS
ACT TWO

PRESET:
  Gift card in envelope on floor near tall stool
    (up stage of steps) with LARRY written on card
  Cut ribbon on Michael's gift (photo)
    (cut so actor can easily break ribbon to get at photo)
  Slit "Boardwalk" tissue paper (makes easier for actor to open)
  Refill ice bucket with ice
  Empty beer can on coffee table (leave one swallow)
  Set bloody bar towel (with styrofoam ice cubes inside)
  Place one "joint" on desk table
  Remove beer can from steps to buffet table (Left)
  Check otto marks and sofa and DR-DL chairs
  Strike—beer can from bar

BEDROOM—2d level
  Place footboard on bed to mask
  Set bedroom bath—2d level—*Off Right*—wet towel
    (Emory's lip)
  Strike from bedroom bath (2d level—*Off Right*)
    Michael's robe
    Donald's airline bag
    Donald's yellow shirt
  Strike from bedroom—*Off Left*—2d level
    Michael's bedroom slippers

OFF STAGE—*Left*—1st level

Fuilly-Fuisse bottle uncapped filled with water

White wine glass*

7 forks

1 knife

Bread basket with 6 rolls covered with red-white check napkin

Wooden salad bowl with shredded lettuce

with wooden fork and spoon for salad

Uncovered casserole (same as Act I covered)

with heated lasagna and serving spoon

Birthday cake with 24 practical white candles*

(this is a fake cake made of 9″ angel food cake tin covered with paper-mache and small rope decorations all painted white)

Kitchen matches

PERSONAL PROPS:

HAROLD—cigarette "joints" (Pall Mall with one end twisted)

EMORY—bloody sweater

COSTUMES

MICHAEL
Charcoal pants
Brown loafers with chain decoration
Beige sweater
Maroon sweater
Red/orange sweater
White shirt with highboy collar and French cuffs
Robe
Slippers
Black knee sox
Cuff links

DONALD
Yellow knit shirt
Navy blue knit shirt
Khaki pants
White sweat sox
White tennis shoes (low; canvas)
Ribbon belt

COWBOY
Blue T-shirt
Pale blue jeans (bleached out)
Cowboy boots
Sox
Red kerchief
Cowboy hat
Wrist strap (black leather)
Birthday card

HANK
Navy blue suit with vest (ivy league)
Black sox
Black shoes (cordovan)
White shirt with French cuffs
Red tie
Cuff links
Belt
Wedding ring

LARRY
Print sheer shirt
Slate grey bell pants
Brown shoes
Sox
Belt

BERNARD
Black pants
Red tie
Black shoes
Black sox
Red/pink oxford shirt (button-down collar)
Black and white tweed jacket

HAROLD—(*this should adjust to latest style*)
Beige Nehru jacket
Brown pants
Brown boots
Sox   } Changed to Edwardian suit
Blue turtleneck T-shirt
Neck chain
sun glasses (metal frames; amber lenses)

EMORY
Yellow sweater
Yellow sweater (with blood)
Plaid Bermuda shorts
Blue tennis shoes (low; canvas)
Sweat sox with red border at top

ALAN
Tuxedo with cummerbund
Tuxedo shirt
Formal bow tie
Black shoes
Black sox
Cuff links
Studs
Wedding ring

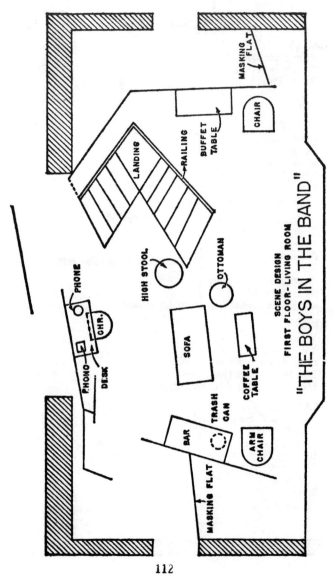

SCENE DESIGN
FIRST FLOOR - LIVING ROOM
"THE BOYS IN THE BAND"